# *Chaser*

## A TWISTED FOX NOVEL

*USA TODAY BESTSELLING AUTHOR*

# CHARITY FERRELL

Visit my website at www.charityferrell.com

Cover Designer: Lori Jackson

Cover Photographer: Lindee Robinson

Editor: Jovana Shirley, Unforeseen Editing, www.unforeseenediting.com

Proofreading: Jenny Sims, Editing for Indies

ISBN-978-1-952496-07-3

# CHAPTER ONE

# Grace

I'M SUING TROJAN.

*Ninety-eight percent effective, my ass.*

Ten tests.

Each one positive.

The only time I want my period, she decides to go on hiatus.

Stupid thing always had bad timing—prom night, spring breaks, recovering from a bad breakup.

I stare at the white stick I'm holding with tears rolling down my cheeks.

Two thin pink lines.

Two reminders of what I did.

*How could I have been so stupid?*

I slept with a man I should've never slept with.

Trusted and fell for a man who was nothing but a heartless, lying asshole.

I'm unsure of how long I've been sitting here, slumped against the tub with the cold tiles hitting the backs of my thighs. I pull my knees to my chest and stare at the truth, wishing I had the power to change it.

A knock on the door breaks me away from my thoughts of regret. Tensing, I grip the stick, and my breath is heavy, as if I'd run a 10K.

*Like that'll ever happen.*

"Grace," Cassidy, my roommate, calls from the other side.

Wiping my snotty nose with my arm, I open my mouth to answer, but no words come. A faint whimper is my only response.

She knocks again. "Are you okay?"

*Hell no.*

*I'm pregnant ... and terrified.*

My overpriced Catholic high school was on to something in their abstinence sex-ed classes when they forced us to watch those childbirth videos. It scarred me for life. Sure, eventually, I planned to marry and have kids. My plan was to at least be prepared and have a partner to share this moment with.

The door slowly opens at my lack of response, and Cassidy slips inside the bathroom. She shuts the door, resting her back against it, and sighs. Concern is etched along her face as our gazes meet.

I sluggishly hold up the stick as if I were seven and Santa had brought me the wrong Barbie for Christmas. "I'm pregnant."

My heart races at my confession.

It's the first time those words have left my mouth.

The first time my secret has been given permission to break into reality.

It'll become my new world, a regular phrase in my vocabulary for the next nine months. Although as my belly grows, that'll be the only evidence people need. Deep down, I know dreading becoming a mother is terrible. I'm a teacher, for Christ's sake. I'm supposed to adore the little rascals, but just because I enjoy children doesn't mean I'm ready to become a single mother. I'll be nursing a baby while nursing my broken heart.

Her soft voice cuts me away from my thoughts. "Is it his?"

I nod. "Unfortunately."

My family is going to kill me.

I'm going to kill him.

The man who swore he was falling in love with me but lied.

The man I wish I could take back ever touching.

The man I thought was different.

# CHAPTER TWO

## Finn

"YOU ASSHOLE!" a drunken idiot yells, the stench of his beer and nacho breath hitting me in the face.

Gripping the back of his shirt, I smirk. "An asshole who's kicking you out."

He grunts and stumbles forward as I forcefully guide him through the bar and outside to the parking lot. I release him, and he turns to flip me off, nearly tripping on his feet. Shaking my head, I chuckle and wait for his ride to pick him up. His friends shove him into the back seat, cursing him for ruining their night, and I wave good-bye before returning to the bar.

Another night, another shift of tossing drunk idiots out of Twisted Fox—the bar where I work. I'm the bouncer, ID checker, and the man who handles any bullshit from customers.

Two guys shove their IDs at me as soon as I'm back at the door, and I step aside, allowing them entry.

There's no stopping a huge-ass grin from taking over my face when the next group comes into view.

I whistle. "There are my favorite girls."

That's not some bullshit compliment babbled with the

hopes of getting laid at the end of the night—a popular move among guys in my line of work. Being a bouncer at bars and clubs gives sway with the ladies.

The compliment is the truth.

The nights are always better when they're here.

What's also the truth? They're off-limits to me.

Georgia, the snarkiest and shortest, is at the front of the line. "Hey, Finney," she says, playfully smacking my stomach.

Behind her is Lola, who winks, and then Cassidy wiggles her fingers in a wave before blowing me a kiss.

I love this group of girls, but no matter what, I have a number one, and tonight, she's at the end of the line.

Save the best for last.

Grace Mitchell.

The only person I'm terrified to love.

The only woman I'm not supposed to crave like I do.

This woman has somehow slipped underneath my skin, rooting her innocence there, and no matter how hard I fight my feelings for her, there's no winning.

She's all I'll ever want and everything I don't deserve.

An alarm rings through me as I look at her, yet she won't do the same with me. Her customary smile—that polite, sweet, and lopsided yet cute-as-fuck grin—is nonexistent and replaced with a deep depth of worry. She walks at a slow pace, and her shoulders are slumped as if being held down by a deep burden.

*What the fuck?*

This isn't my Grace.

I stop her before she passes me. "Damn, babe, bad day?"

"Bad week," she mutters, fidgeting with the strap of her designer handbag.

Just as I'm about to ask why, Georgia says, "Let's grab our table before my favorite is stolen."

Cassidy laughs. "Your favorite, meaning the one closest to your man?"

"Damn straight." Georgia smirks at her. "Don't act like it's not close to *your* boyfriend too."

Lola gestures toward their usual table. "Silas is already saving it for us."

Neglecting my job and not giving a shit—*sorry, bosses* (aka my friends who won't fire me)—I follow them to the table. On my way, I direct another employee to take my place. The girls slide out their stools, plopping down one by one. As soon as Grace's ass hits her seat, she bows her head, her strawberry-blond hair creating a wall of curls around her face.

My gut twists from seeing her like this. Squeezing between her and Georgia, I tip my head and whisper in Grace's ear, "What happened?"

"Nothing," she rushes out.

Georgia slaps her hand on the table. "All right, give me your margarita orders."

Everyone blurts out their flavor but Grace.

"Just a water for me," she replies, her voice soft.

"No margarita?" Georgia asks, raising a brow.

Margarita nights are a weekly tradition for them. Not only that, but it's also her go-to when she's having a shit day.

"I wish," Grace replies before slapping a hand over her mouth and shutting her eyes. She quickly changes her tone. "I work in the morning."

Lola checks her watch. "Babe, you look like you've had a hell of a day. Have a drink, scarf down some greasy bar food, and don't give a shit about calories. Consider it a serotonin booster." She winks at her. "Trust me, I'm a pro at this stuff."

Grace drops her hand to her stomach. "Maybe another time."

"Whoa," Silas says from the stool next to Lola. "You knocked up or something?"

Leave it to Silas to ask a stupid-ass question like that.

No one laughs.

The table goes silent with the exception of Cassidy breaking out in a fit of coughs. Grace chews on her upper lip as I edge in closer to her. I wait for her to deny it, to tell Silas he's ridiculous, to laugh it off.

She doesn't.

As corny as it sounds, my heart stops. Hell, my entire world stops. The sounds of customers yelling at sports calls on the TVs and mindless chatter surrounding me fade. Squeezing my eyes shut, I pray this is a bad nightmare, that I drank too much last night and I'm hallucinating, or this is some prank. Everyone's reactions tell me my wish isn't coming true.

It could be considered selfish of me to not want to hear Grace is pregnant. For years, I've carried a deep fear of losing her. Her being pregnant with another man's baby is step one of that looming reality—of my upcoming loss of the woman I never want to disappear from my life.

My world, my happiness will never be the same.

# CHAPTER THREE

# Grace

ONE THING my parents loved about me while I was growing up was I almost always told the truth. No matter how much a lie was on the tip of my tongue, it never slipped.

*Did you participate in senior skip day? Yes.*

*Did you attend a party instead of going to Georgia's after prom? Sure did.*

*Did you cheer on Lola to put a laxative in your ex's drink after he took your virginity and then cheated? Unfortunately, yes, and by the way, he's threatening to sue.*

That's why I can't look my friends in the face and deny being pregnant.

*Was I that obvious?*

I hadn't bailed tonight in hopes it'd take my mind off being knocked up. With the exception of work, I hadn't left my house since accepting the results of the tests. I had anxiety that someone would know my secret as soon as they saw me.

*Or as soon as I declined a margarita, apparently.*

All eyes are on me.

*God, if you're listening, please open up the floor and swallow me whole.*

I'm not sure how long it takes before I draw in a nervous breath and nod. I shut my eyes to block out their reactions, afraid of what they'll be. A crowded bar isn't where I planned to spill the beans, but at least it's over with.

Another name off my list.

*Friends. Check.*

The others, like my family and the baby's father, won't be as easy.

And unfortunately, I can't have a margarita with those either.

"Who's the father?" Finn asks, his voice pained and cracking with each word.

Yeah, I'd rather give up margs for the rest of my life before explaining that tonight.

Out of everyone, his reaction is what I've been worried about the most. As much as I like the other guys, I don't care about their opinions. The girls will support me one hundred percent—there's no question.

I could lie and say IVF, but my friends would call bullshit, knowing I'd never keep something like that a secret. Nor can I say I turned into the next Virgin Mary and got prego without having intercourse.

My head spins, a myriad of excuses flashing through my thoughts, but I'm unable to grasp one.

I clear my throat. "I don't want to talk about that."

Questions fly from people's mouths, but Lola shoots her hand up, stopping them.

"She'll talk about it when she's ready," she says, smiling in my direction before sending Finn a *shut the hell up* glare.

That's Lola—always the first to speak up and the first to shut people down.

"Do your parents know?" Georgia asks.

"Not yet," I croak, my throat sore.

Georgia shifts in her stool, her hand falling over mine and

squeezing it. "Do you want me to go with you when you tell them? I mean, I'm down for being a second mom."

This is why I love my friends. Along with my older sister, Faith, they will be the strength I need to get through this and prove I'm not alone.

I can't muster the courage to turn and look at Finn. From his tense muscles and his heavy breathing, I'm scared of witnessing the disappointment I know is written on his face.

The anger.

And possible disgust.

Even though he and I have never overstepped our friendship line, we share an emotional intimacy that we deny it to everyone. We've surpassed friendship. When I met Finn, I didn't expect us to develop the connection we have. I never anticipated this man, who was the complete opposite of me, to steal my heart, taking it little by little with every conversation until he owned every inch of it. And since neither of us planned our relationship to grow as it has, we're terrified to admit our feelings to each other, so we've been playing pretend for years.

I'm in love with Finn. If there were anyone I'd want to be the father of my baby, it'd be him. In my dreams, if I could have my life any way I wanted, I'd be with Finn. I've had those feelings for years, but sometimes, you can't always have what you want.

After longing for Finn while witnessing endless women flirt with him at the bar, I stupidly attempted to move on. I threw myself into a relationship even though my heart belonged to someone else. I wanted to find happiness without the fear of cutting myself open and confessing my feelings to Finn, scared of being shut down, of hearing I wasn't his type.

I'm in love with him, my best friend, and it's too bad the other man's heart also belongs to someone else. He was running from his problems, his responsibilities, and used me. Unfortunately, I found that out too late.

And that man, ladies and gentlemen, is the father of my baby.

# CHAPTER FOUR

# Finn

THE FIRST THING I do at closing is march behind the bar, snag a bottle of whiskey, and pour myself a double.

*Pregnant.*

*Grace is fucking pregnant.*

I had no idea she was even dating someone, and from her reaction when I asked who the father was, the dick had probably fucked her over. Unless it was a one-night stand and she doesn't know who the father is, but for as long as I've known Grace, I can't see that being the answer.

My goal is to drink away the reality until it's no longer fresh in my mind. I'm using the liquor to cope with the pain of losing her. I cringe, thinking of some underserving asshole touching her, kissing her, doing everything I've wanted to do for years.

"You good, man?" Silas comes up behind me and slaps me on the back.

It's all fun and games, joking about someone being pregnant, until it's the girl you're in love with.

When Grace confirmed she was pregnant, Silas looked straight at me, knowing it'd hit me the hardest. I knotted my hands into fists, nausea crawling up my throat, wishing I hadn't followed them to their table. That's what I get for being a shit employee and not minding my damn business.

After her pregnancy news broke, I got back to work. My head was spinning, and I needed to clear it. I shot quick glances to their table throughout the night, watching her drink water and pretend to laugh. Her face was tired when she left the bar, and before she walked out, I smacked a quick kiss on her forehead and reminded her I would always be there for her, no matter what.

This is just another reminder that Grace and I were never meant to be together. I'm not sure how it happened, but I've connected with her more than anyone in our small group. We get along, share stories, and spend every minute we can together. I should've known something was up because we've started drifting apart for the past few months. Now, I know why.

"All good," I clip, taking another drink to drown out my lie.

He snatches the bottle from me. "Don't bullshit me."

"Would you be pissed if you found out Lola was pregnant?"

He looks away. "I don't know."

"Bullshit." I mock the tone he used with me. "You would."

He sighs. "Let me drive you home."

Before he can stop me, I pluck the bottle from his hand and take a long draw. Passing it back nearly empty, I gulp. "Let's go."

This is my hell. All these years, I've convinced myself that Grace is too good for me, but I've always turned a blind eye to what would happen if I never made my move. What would happen if another man had bigger balls than me and asked her out.

In the back of my mind, I stupidly believed we'd stay friends forever and nothing would ever change. Sure, we've gone on dates—neither one of us staying celibate, *obviously*—but nothing ever turned serious.

We shut the bar down, and as soon as I fall into his passenger seat, I text Grace.

**Me: You okay?**

Since she wakes up early for her job, I don't expect a response back until morning. I'm shocked when three bubbles pop up on the screen, and a text comes through.

**Grace. Yes. Just tired.**

**Me: I'm here for you. Don't forget that, okay?**

**Grace: I know.**

**Me: Always. Get some rest.**

**Grace: *heart emoji***

My heart stings, and I tip my head back, regret eating at me. *Why did I wait?*

*It's too late now.*

All I can do now is be there for her.

No matter what happens, no matter how much it kills me inside, I'll always be at her side for as long as she needs me. Rain or shine, day or night, until she moves on with a man who isn't too chickenshit to let her all the way in.

"Try not to think about it," Silas says, parking in front of my condo. "Block that shit out because there's nothing you can do now." He taps the center console. "Go to bed because you look like shit."

"Rest?" I snort. "Doubt that'll happen." Clutching the door handle, I nod toward him. "Thanks for the ride, man."

"Anytime."

I take two steps at a time, surprised I can even walk, and it takes me a few attempts to open the door. Slamming the door behind me, I dart to the kitchen for the vodka bottle stashed in the top cabinet before plopping down on the couch in the living room. I take a shot of vodka at the same time I grab the remote with my free hand. Groaning, I toss the remote on the floor, not in the mood for background noise. It'll be me, silence, and my broken heart tonight.

I stupidly thought Grace and I would have a chance someday.

When I had my shit together, when I was more than a bouncer in a bar, when I could provide her with the life she'd always been given.

Waiting is for fools.

What a goddamn mistake that was.

Now, I'm paying for it.

# CHAPTER FIVE

# Grace

I HAVEN'T HAD a good night's sleep since I was thirteen, but last night was the worst I'd had since moving out of my parents' home.

I'm yawning on my way to the kitchen when there's a knock on the door. Making a detour, I check the peephole before answering it. Finn stands in front of me, his eyes heavy-lidded and his ashen-brown hair disheveled.

Apparently, I'm not the only one suffering from a lack of sleep.

A green smoothie is gripped in one of his hands, and in the other is a brown bag, both items sporting the logo of my favorite breakfast café. I stare at him, blinking, shocked he's even awake. He works late and tends to sleep in until noon. Just like he never expects a text from me past eleven, I never expect one from him until lunch.

He fakes a smile and holds up the bag. "I thought you could use a good breakfast this morning."

I return the smile—mine not fraudulent. It's the first real one I've had in days.

"I can't believe you're up this early," I say, motioning for him to come inside.

"Neither can I." Walking in, he follows me to the kitchen, hands me the smoothie, and settles the bag onto the counter before rubbing his eyes. "I couldn't sleep."

"Why?"

He shrugs. "Probably the same reason you couldn't." His eyes widen, and his next words are rushed. "I didn't mean for that to make me sound like a rude asshole."

I'm not offended by his honesty. You take one look at me and know I'm lacking sleep. Circles that I was too exhausted to cover up with makeup are under my eyes. My pink dress is one that's shoved in the back of my closet, only used for *I'm feeling bloated* days.

"Finn"—I sigh—"please don't worry about me. I got this. I'm a big girl."

"Don't worry about you?" He throws his arms in the air in frustration. "All I'm going to do is worry about you. Will the father be in the picture?"

"I ... I haven't told him yet."

That's on today's ... or tomorrow's ... or next year's ... or never's to-do list.

He rubs at his brows, but his stare doesn't slip away from me. "Why?"

"Right now, I don't even want to look at him."

He moves his hand, his face reddening. "Did he hurt you?"

*Only emotionally.*

"No," I reply. "It's nothing like that."

"Has hell frozen over?"

I turn around at Cassidy's voice as she joins us in the kitchen.

Another person who normally doesn't wake up this early.

Her blonde hair is a mess, and she's sporting one of her boyfriend's tees.

"Finn, what are you doing up?" she asks, her gaze from Finn to me before stopping on him. "Please tell me you slept over."

"Nah." Finn shakes his head. "I just brought Grace breakfast before work."

Cassidy's attention shifts to me, giving my appearance a once-over. "Don't take this the wrong way, babe, but I think you're due for a sick day. I'll take one with you."

"I'm down for a sick day," Finn says.

"Me fucking too," Lincoln, Cassidy's boyfriend, says, coming into view.

*Looks like this is a breakfast party.*

*I want my non-prego peace-and-quiet mornings back.*

As much as a relief taking the day off would be, it's too late for that. Plus, I have decisions I need to make, and one of them requires me showing up to work.

I blow out a breath. "I can't call in sick thirty minutes before I'm supposed to be there."

"You know, you can quit if you want," Lincoln says, shoving his hands into the pockets of his sweats. "We're good to cover rent."

Since Lincoln was with Cassidy the night she came into the bathroom and nearly lives with us, he was the second person to find out about my pregnancy. Like Cassidy, he kept his word on keeping it a secret. Also like Cassidy, he knows who the father is.

"Why would you quit your job?" Finn asks.

Lincoln and Cassidy exchange a look.

"Just ... stress," I rush out, not exactly lying to him.

Being there, being around *him*, will be stressful.

He nods, although there's still a question in his eyes. He'll wait for the answer until we're alone. One thing I appreciate about Finn is that he never puts me on the spot and always makes sure I'm comfortable.

We make small talk before Finn grabs my breakfast bag and

walks me to my Mercedes coupe. Our pace is quick and hurried. I set my purse into the passenger seat, rest the cup in the holder, and turn back to look at him.

He fixes his gaze on me as if attempting to crack answers without asking questions.

Endeavoring to *read me* without making me uncomfortable.

Reaching out, he brushes away a strand of my hair waving in the wind. "Don't forget, you need anything, and I'm here."

"I know." I bow my head. "I know."

He hugs me good-bye.

Finn and I share two types of hugs.

Our friendly ones—him casually throwing his arm over my shoulders in a playful manner.

And our deep ones—him blanketing me in his arms, as if he's my protector, and holding me tight.

Today's is a deep one.

And as I'm bundled in his arms, I wish it would last forever.

---

I WALK into Sunset Hill Preparatory with a slow pace, my throat tightening with doubt.

I've taught third grade here for two years. It's an elite school with tuition costing nearly as much as an Ivy League.

I wave at Rachelle, the secretary, as I enter the office and hope my voice doesn't sound scratchy. "Morning! Is Principal Long in his office?"

*Is this the right place to do this?*

Probably not, but I don't want to meet him in private anywhere.

*The less time with him, the better.*

He also can't make a scene here.

So, the school it is.

She grins from ear to ear at his name. "Sure is!"

Rachelle is a big fan of the principal.

Most at Sunset Hill are—staff, parents, students.

The man succeeds at faking it.

My hand trembles when I knock on the door. I'm close to changing my mind, to flee, when he yells for me to come in.

"You can do this," I whisper to myself, avoiding Rachelle's gaze, worried she'll notice my nervousness.

I'm proud of myself when I open the door and step inside. I glance back at the door, debating on whether to shut it. It's something I was always hesitant about in the past—closing us in and people speculating we were up to no good. This moment is similar … although something different will be happening this time.

Sitting behind the mahogany desk is a man I once adored yet now think is trash. He looks the part in his black suit and fun tie; his brown hair is curly yet controlled simultaneously.

A flash of shock quickly passes over his features at the sight of me.

He smirks and jerks his head toward the door—a silent demand to shut it, and I do. "And here I thought you were done with me." Leaning forward, he steeples his hands and rests them over a stack of paperwork on the desk.

Gone is the nice-guy front he delivered for months.

*Why is it always the quiet, polite ones who end up being the most deceitful?*

As much as I've frowned upon players, at least they're open about their intentions.

I raise my chin. "I am."

"Why are you here then?" The satisfaction in his tone confirms he assumes this is me running back to him.

He licks his lips while eyeing me in expectation.

*Here goes.*

"I'm pregnant." I'm proud of how sharp my tone is—no stuttering, no doubt.

The smirk he was carrying drops faster than his morals. "Motherfucker." His face pales as he slides his chair out from the desk and stands. "This can't be happening."

"I don't expect anything from you," I rush out, nearly pleading. "You can sign over your rights, and I'll raise the baby on my own."

I swallow at the thought of doing it alone, but as terrifying as single motherhood sounds, I'll take that over having Gavin in my life.

He rubs the back of his neck. "No, that's not what I want."

*Wait, what?*

Not what I expected.

"You know what you're saying, right?" My words come out slow, as if I were speaking to one of my students.

He nods. "I do."

"You'd have to come clean to your wife." I squeeze my eyes shut at the last word.

It's a hidden detail of his life.

A label he kept in the dark.

There was no ring. No photos. No social media.

All I had was his word ... or lack thereof.

I assumed he didn't have a wife since he never made it clear he did.

"Not exactly." He clicks his tongue against the roof of his mouth while circling the desk to come closer.

I grimace as he draws near. "I'm confused."

"My wife ..." He clears his throat and stands tall in front of me, the sage tones in his cologne hitting my nose. "She's also pregnant."

I swing my hand back, prepared to punch him, but hold back.

*This motherfucking asshole.*

Curse words aren't a regular in my vocabulary.

Since I'm around children all day, I've trained myself to use kid-friendly language.

But this ... this calls for profanity.

And a quick kick in the balls if being fired wasn't a consequence.

"Did you ..." I retreat a step and signal between us, begging tears not to surface. "When did *you know*?"

*When we had sex?*

*Exchanged love devotions?*

*Had sleepovers at his temporary condo?*

He tugs at his ear, his eyes leveled on mine and lips pinched together. "That doesn't matter. If she finds out I cheated, our prenup will be null and void. No way in hell am I giving her half of the money my family worked their asses off for." The disdain on his face disintegrates, his mood changing, and he smiles. "I want to be with you, Grace. I love *you*, not her."

Reaching out, he attempts to take my hand, but I swat his away.

Snarling, I shove my finger in his face. "Don't. Don't you dare. You no longer get to touch me. You lost that privilege when you failed to tell me you were married."

Gavin recently relocated to Anchor Ridge, Iowa, from California to take the job as principal here. His wife wanted his children to finish out the semester at their old school and decided to join him later. Temporarily, he rented a small condo while waiting for them. Not once did he mention a wife, so I never questioned it.

Along with most of the staff, I found out about his family when his wife showed up at the school to surprise him. As I dropped my bagel to the floor while processing what was happening, the warning signs I'd missed became clear. The times he had taken calls in different rooms with hushed whispers and how he'd hardly mentioned his life in California.

His mouth falls slack at my rejection. "There is something between us."

This time, when he takes a step closer, I don't move as if frozen in place. Reaching out, he runs his soft palm over my face, and I tremble.

"We were falling in love, remember? Those feelings aren't something that can just be thrown away ... forgotten."

Him lowering his hand to swipe a finger along my top lip snaps me back into reality, and he stumbles back when I push his chest.

"Maybe, but I'd never be with a married man," I hiss.

"What if I was no longer married?" He shakes his head. "Let me figure out a way to get out of this marriage without it being messy. Then, we can be together and have a perfect life."

"No way. I shouldn't have even told you I'm pregnant."

He raises a brow. "Why did you?"

"I'm a good person, and keeping something like this from someone would be wrong. But I forgot it's you—a manipulative jerk. Go be with your wife or don't be—I don't care. Anything that was ever between us is over."

He snarls, pointing to my stomach. The man changes moods as much as he lies. "That's my unborn child, which means I have rights as a father. I don't intend to give those up."

My stomach clenches.

I was trying to do the right thing, but it's backfired in my face. Since he's such a shitty person, I thought he'd want nothing to do with this baby.

"You want rights?" I ask. "Go tell your wife because sooner or later, those rights will result in her knowing about us."

He goes quiet.

I snort. "That's what I thought."

With that, I open the door and walk out.

# CHAPTER SIX

## Finn

THE RINGING PHONE wakes me up, and I groan when reading the name across the screen.

The past twenty-four hours since finding out Grace is pregnant have been a roller coaster of emotions. I'm still trying to get my head on straight, and now, I'll have the added stress of this call. But like always, I answer.

I answer out of fear of what will happen if I don't. "Hello?"

"Hey, son." His chipper tone should be a relief, but all it tells me is, he's about to ask for money.

I pinch the bridge of my nose. "What's going on?"

"Oh, nothing," he drawls out his response as if preparing himself to break the news. "My car broke down, and I can't afford to fix it."

Just as I thought.

Saving money is nearly impossible because I'm always handing it out like candy. I'm not a selfish man, and I'm always down to lend a helping hand to those down on their luck. My issue is supporting someone who blows through their Social Security checks on booze and drugs and then comes to me when he can't pay his bills.

"Take it to the shop." I shut my eyes, hating myself for enabling him. "Have them call me. I'll either go there or pay it over the phone."

He grunts. "I'll come by and pick up the money. It'll be easier that way."

"No." My voice turns stern. "We do it my way, or it doesn't get paid."

"Fine," he grumbles. "You always make it difficult when it could be easy and save you the trouble."

It's a trick I've fallen victim to countless times. Me handing him money in these situations, resulting in him conveniently *losing it* or having an excuse of how he had to pay for something else. The man once claimed the hundred-dollar bill I'd once given him blew away in the wind like it was a damn kite. It's been this way for as long as I can remember, and I don't expect it to change anytime soon.

---

TACO TUESDAY IS my favorite day of the week.

As someone who grew up with no family, what drags me out of a sour mood is my friends. For once in this fucked-up life of mine, I'm not lonely 24/7. I have people who care about me, who I care about, relationships that weren't created to see what someone could get out of me.

I met Cohen while we worked at a club in the city together. Over the years, we built a tight circle, consisting of Cohen, Silas, Archer, Maliki, and myself. After we met, Cohen introduced us to his sister, Georgia, and her friends, Lola and Grace. Later, Cassidy and Lincoln started working at the bar, and our group was complete.

Meeting Grace changed my life. I'd never met anyone like her. She had the smile of purity, an angelic voice, but her personality was what drew me in. There was no doubt she was high maintenance, someone who had come from money, but she had no problem casually hanging out with us at barbecues and shooting the shit. She was a breath of fresh air.

I won't lie. In the beginning, I judged her for her privileged life—her Mercedes and the way she talked like she hung out in country clubs during her summers—but she proved my ass wrong.

Taco Tuesday is being held at Archer, Georgia, and Lincoln's penthouse. Technically, it's pretty much Lincoln's because Archer and Georgia recently bought another home that's more Georgia's style. Not that he stays there much either since he practically lives at Cassidy and Grace's.

I press my palm to my heart when I walk in and see Grace sitting on the couch, surrounded by our friends. She turns, her eyes meeting mine, and shoots me a sweet grin.

That damn smile.

My favorite fucking view.

I could live with that being the only sight I see for the rest of my life, and I'd be one happy man. The penthouse is an open floor plan, so I see everyone scattered throughout the place. On my way to Grace, I wave to people in the kitchen and high-five Cohen's son, Noah. After saying hi to everyone, I plop down next to Grace on the couch. I squeeze Grace's thigh—a silent question that she's okay—and she nods.

"The margaritas are ready!" Georgia shouts, walking into the living room, a frozen drink in each hand, and she hands one over to Grace. "And a virgin one for my girl, so you're not left out."

Grace laughs while taking it from her.

"What's *a virgin one* mean?" Noah asks, scrunching his brows.

"It means ..." Jamie—Cohen's girlfriend/baby mama—says before pausing, searching for the right words.

"It means it doesn't have alcohol in it," Georgia says, using her free hand to ruffle his brown hair.

Noah perks up. "Does that mean when I drink chocolate milk, I'm drinking virgin chocolate milk?"

"Oh my God," Jamie says, facepalming. "That is not where he needs to go with this."

"And what about milkshakes?" Noah goes on. "Are they virgin milkshakes?"

"I'm going to kill all of you," Jamie says, using her finger to gesture to us. "All of you will be drinking virgin margaritas during our Taco Tuesday nights." She peers at Grace and winks. "Get ready for those questions in five years."

Grace's face pales, and I give her thigh another squeeze.

Every minute I can, I want to make sure she's comfortable. She's venturing into a rough journey, and I'll be there for her every step she'll allow me.

Even if it hurts because I wish I were the father, that I'd stepped up and told her my feelings. Now, all I can do is be a support system, a friend, a man who wishes she were his.

———

I DON'T GET a moment alone with Grace until after dinner.

With the exception of the few minutes we had before being interrupted at her townhouse, we haven't had a full conversation since her pregnancy news broke.

We're back on the couch after stuffing ourselves with tacos and guac.

There are so many questions I want to ask, yet so many I don't want to know the answers to.

*Tell me about how it happened, but I don't want to know that you had sex with another man. Explain how you kept a relationship from me, but also don't tell me shit about him.*

I might not know the dude, but I hate him.

I've done a decent job of playing it cool tonight, but finally, I can release the anxiousness that's been eating away at me. My attention is fixed on her, not taking in any of the motions or conversations around us. Her hair is pulled up, exposing her slim neck. I shut my eyes, remembering the first time I saw her. As weird as it sounds, the color of her hair reminded me of fruit —a mixture of apricot and strawberries.

She changed from her work clothes—her teacher outfits, as I call them—and she's wearing striped overalls. They're not Farmer Ben overalls—more along the lines of what you'd see a celebrity sporting on the front page of a magazine. It fits her skinny frame, the cream color and blue stripes beautiful against her sun-kissed skin.

"How are you feeling?" I ask, blowing out a stressed breath.

She sighs, avoiding eye contact. "I told the father."

"And?" My heart races.

*Do I even want to know?*

Her answer could make or break us.

*If she got together with the baby daddy, would he want me around?*

*Or would he see me as a threat?*

If the roles were reversed, I know I would.

Anyone who watches Grace and me together knows that we're not just friends, no matter how much we lie to each other about it.

She plays with her hands in her lap. "He wants to be in the baby's life."

*Fuck, this stings.*

"Is that what you want?"

"Not exactly. I mean ... yes ... but no."

I scratch my head. "What do you mean?"

Moments of silence pass as she chews into her cheek.

Her hands stop, and she looks forward. "He's married."

My mouth drops open.

Not what I expected.

*This motherfucker.*

Her shoulders slump. "Married ... with children ... and another one on the way."

Anger swells inside me, but I draw in steady breaths to hold myself back from acting on it. I thought I had questions before, but this? This is an entirely different field.

She eyes me nervously. "I didn't know he was married. He hid it from me."

Scrubbing a hand over my face, I appear as stressed as her. "What are you going to do?" I wrap my arm around her shoulders, drawing her into my side. "Are you sure you don't want to take me up on the offer of kicking his ass?"

At this point, if I knew who the bastard was, I'd do it without asking. It'd feel damn good to smash my fist into a man's face who lied, played, and knocked up the most important woman in my life.

She relaxes into my hold. "No, it'll only make the situation worse."

"Did he tell his wife?"

"As of yesterday, nope."

"He thinks he can hide it from her?"

This dude has some serious balls.

"I have no idea." She frowns. "My guess is, he wants to be in the baby's life because he wants to keep me."

I grind my teeth.

"But I think he'll chicken out when it's time to tell his wife, and then the baby and I will be on our own." Her eyes squeeze shut.

I carefully take her hand in mine. "You're strong, and you won't be on your own. You have me. You have our friends."

A tear falls down her cheek, and she bows her head. "My

sister lost so many friends after she had my niece. It changes things."

"What's wrong, babe?" Georgia asks, taking a seat on the floor at Grace's feet and crossing her legs.

As much as our friends bring joy into my life, they have terrible timing. They have no problem with interrupting conversations and calling people out.

Grace swipes the tear from her rosy cheek. "I'm just thinking about doing it all alone if the dad doesn't want to be in the picture."

"Um, you have me," Georgia counters.

"And *me* in the next room," Cassidy chimes in, walking toward us with the group following behind her.

"You have *all of us*," Lola adds. "Every step of the way, we'll be there for you. I'm totally up for Lamaze class, and we all know Georgia is the queen of positivity. She'll be at your side every step of the way, holding your hand through labor. We can take turns being the baby daddy, and one day, you'll find a man ready to step up and take over our job."

"I'm down for playing baby daddy for a few days," Silas says, pointing at Grace with his beer.

Grace's mood doesn't improve. "That's if I'm alive when my parents find out."

"It's the twenty-first century. We're in new times," Cohen says. "Even if they're upset at first, they'll get over it because they love you."

Georgia reaches up and squeezes Grace's knee. "We got this, babe."

———————

"YOU KNOW, I was thinking about something," Silas says.

He and I, along with Georgia and Archer, who are in the kitchen, are the only ones left in the penthouse. It wasn't long after our conversation with Grace not going on her journey alone that she went home.

I snort. "That's fucking scary."

"I have the perfect plan for Grace and her baby."

"Not taking any advice from the guy who suggested we have an adults-only baby shower at the club."

He rolls his eyes before pointing at me. "You step up and be the dad."

I should've known better than to take a drink before he spoke because as soon as the words leave his mouth, I'm choking on my beer. Dribbles scatter along my shirt as I gawk at him. Silas is the jokester of the group, and I expect a sarcastic smirk on his face. There isn't.

"I can't tell if you're joking or serious," I grunt, wiping my palm down my shirt.

He chuckles. "Eh, kind of both. Although leaning more toward serious."

"For someone who doesn't drink, you sure say some drunk-person bullshit."

"The least you can do is act like it in front of her parents. The poor girl looked stressed as fuck when she mentioned them."

I shift in my seat. "And what? Be a dad for a day?"

"Go with her, introduce yourself as the dad, and then later, she can say you broke up." He delivers a self-satisfied smirk. "*Or*, better yet, maybe this is the moment you've been waiting for. Have a relationship with her and be fucking happy."

I chug the rest of my beer. "You're nuts, dude."

"Are you honestly going to lie and deny you want to be with her?"

My jaw clenches at his truth. "Oh, like you haven't wanted a relationship with Lola for years and not done shit about it?"

He leans back in his chair, slouching some, and I know my

words hit a nerve. "Lola and I would never work. We're too much alike."

"Grace and I are too different."

"Keep lying to yourself, dude, and be fucking miserable for the rest of your life." He holds his bottle of water in a cheers gesture before standing and walking away.

As I get in my car and leave, Silas's comment sticks with me.

# CHAPTER SEVEN

## Grace

I'M NOT sure what's worse.

Finding out your boyfriend is trash or morning sickness.

Screw you both.

You're already going through enough during pregnancy—hormone changes, weight gain, peeing your pants on occasion. Why throw *get sick every morning* into the mix? Give us a break on something.

My sister complained about morning sickness during her pregnancy, and I passed it off, thinking it was normal. I sincerely apologize to anyone who's ever had someone downplay the hell.

It's brutal.

Disgusting.

Resting my head on the toilet, I groan.

This isn't how my mid-twenties was supposed to go.

After rinsing my mouth and brushing my teeth three times, I shower and get ready for work. Another day of avoiding my baby daddy at every turn.

IF I'M EVER LATE, call the cops.

Nothing good comes out of tardiness.

Shoot, my late period proved that further.

Growing up, I was taught if you're not early, you're late. As the daughter of a judge, I grew up with manners that were expected to be on display and rules that were never to be broken. It's not that my parents are jerks. It's just that they're strict, and they have had expectations of us since childhood.

College. Job. Marriage. Children.

In that order.

My sister performed well.

Me? Apparently, I'm rearranging those expectations.

I'm at my desk thirty minutes early, grading papers and sipping on seltzer water before my class starts. At times, especially now, I appreciate silence before the chaos that begins with children shuffling into the room.

"Wow, babe, you look gorgeous today."

I straighten in my chair, a chill shooting up my spine.

*That voice.*

His presence now is so different than what it was when we met ... when he was charming me. Gone is the phony compassion and sweetness, now replaced with arrogance. For someone whose life could change if I confessed the truth, he sure has some balls.

Knocking on the door with his knuckles, Gavin stands in the doorway. "Pregnancy shines on you."

My head pounds as Gavin shuts the door and strolls toward me, a smirk on his face. Nausea thicker than my morning sickness creeps up my throat.

*How'd I allow him to fool me?*

Infatuation is blinding, ladies and gents.

"Screw you," I hiss, dropping my pen.

He places his hand over his chest. "Aw, you used to appreciate my compliments."

"*Used to* being the key words. Now, they make my skin crawl because I know they're coming from a married man." I scowl while pointing at the door. "Get out."

"I'm the principal." He scrubs a hand over his smooth jaw and smirks. "My job is to ensure you're doing yours and there are no issues."

"My only issue is you."

"Now, now, is that any way to talk to your superior?" He stops in front of me, his palms falling to my desk, and bends so we're eye level. A combination of his spearmint breath and strong cologne floats between us.

I snort—convinced if I don't entertain him, he'll leave.

"Or better yet, the father of your child?"

My face burns, and I hold myself back from slapping him in the face. "Don't say that to taunt me."

He draws nearer, our faces only inches apart. "The truth taunts you?"

"*You* taunt me." It's a struggle to stop my voice from wavering. "Your asshole attitude taunts me. Being around you taunts me."

Typically, I don't resort to insults, but he deserves it. Gavin lied, made me fall for him, all while knowing it'd all come crashing down. He didn't care that I was playing victim to his lies while he was having fun.

He was a pro at it. The man excelled at hiding what he wanted, so my bet is, I'm not the first affair he's had. I was stupid. In today's day and age, you're supposed to cyberstalk potential new love interests—look through every Instagram photo, see how cute their exes dress, and discover their political views.

The problem was that Gavin declared social media a waste of time, but I also trusted him. We worked together, and the school is strict on background checks. It wasn't like I could ask around since we agreed to keep our relationship private for a while. I was scared of it ending before things got serious and there'd be talk around the school.

It ending too soon was my fear.

Not him being married.

I grip the edge of my desk, pushing my chair out, and stand. "Out of my room."

His back straightens as he pulls away, standing tall and slender in front of me. "Oh, come on, Grace." He approaches me. "I told you, I'm leaving my wife, but for now, let's go back to the way it was. Remember how good we were?" He shuts his eyes as if the memories are so good, but all they do is haunt me.

I shove him away. "All I remember is that you're a cheating jerk."

"Forgive me." He presses his hands into a praying motion. "I saw you, I wanted you, but I knew if you found out I was married, you'd want nothing to do with me."

"You think?" I scoff.

He opens his mouth, most likely to spew more lies, but a group of children barreling into the classroom interrupts him. Pulling away, he says, "Have a great day, Miss Mitchell. Until next time."

---

"YOU LOOK like someone ran over Mr. Bubbles," my sister, Faith, says when I enter her kitchen.

Her signature candle—honeydew melon—is lit in the center of the granite island, a relaxation to my anxiety. The irritation from Gavin's morning visit stayed with me. All day, I stared at the door, waiting for him to make another pop-in.

Brian, her husband, chuckles. "Grace would probably kill someone if they ran over Mr. Bubbles."

Mr. Bubbles is the stuffed rabbit I carried around until I was ten and still have to this day. There's something about safekeeping childhood objects. My plan was to pass him down to my children. Looks like that time is coming sooner than I thought.

"I'm pregnant," I blurt out, unable to hold my secret in any longer.

Faith and I share everything. Keeping information from her is hard.

"I'm sorry, but did you just say you're *pregnant*?" Faith gapes at me as if waiting for me to tell her I'm joking.

I clear my throat. "I'm pregnant."

As nervous as I was to tell her, a rush of relief settles through me now that she finally knows. Her support will mean so much to me during this journey, and she's the closest person to me who's been pregnant.

"Whoa," Brian says, his tone subdued.

"Is this a good or bad *I'm pregnant*?" Faith stares at me in expectation. "Because you most definitely don't look like I did when I found out I was pregnant."

Chewing on my lower lip, I walk to the fridge, jerk it open, snag a bottle of water, and chug half of it.

All eyes are on me. The knife that was in Faith's hand while she chopped onions sits on the counter, and Brian is no longer holding his phone.

"I don't know if I want to answer that." I slump back against the fridge. "I don't want to say something negative and have my baby pick up bad vibes, yet I don't want to say good because I'm freaking the heck out."

"Who's the father?" she asks.

*God, I hate that question.*

I squeeze the bottle tight, wishing it were Gavin's balls. "I don't want to talk about it."

Her gaze is glued to me. "Is it one of the guys you and Georgia always hang out with?"

"No." I shut my eyes. "It's someone I work with."

"Why the long face then?"

Even though I just drained a bottle of water, my mouth turns dry. "It recently came to light that he's married—"

"Oh fuck," Brian says.

"And he's also expecting another child with said wife." My stomach revolts at the confession.

"Holy shit," Faith hisses, tapping her French-manicured nails along the counter. "Good luck explaining that one to Mom and Dad."

Brian points his beer at me. "Please make sure we're in attendance."

Faith playfully smacks the side of Brian's head.

"Who knows?" I drag out a stool and collapse onto it. "Maybe it won't be so bad."

"I have an idea," Brian says. "Buy your mom a Chanel bag and slide the ultrasound picture in there." He cracks a cocky smile. "No one can be pissed when they've been gifted an expensive-ass handbag."

I rub my forehead. "Chanel won't drown out an unwed pregnancy."

Brian snorts. "Surely, your parents don't believe you don't have sex."

Faith shoots me a smile. "Grace is an angel in their eyes."

"They thought the same thing about you." I wiggle my finger in her direction.

"Angel, my ass," Brian mutters, finishing off his beer.

"It was you who corrupted me." She points him in the direction of the chilled wine on the counter. "Now, pour me a glass of that, so I can help my sister come up with a plan."

Brian salutes her before doing as she said.

"Drink in front of the pregnant woman," I mutter. "That'll sure make me feel better."

"Hey, my best ideas come when I've had a few glasses,"

Faith says. "All I'm saying is that Mom and Dad will find out sooner or later. You can't exactly hide being pregnant."

I tap the corner of my mouth before pointing at her. "What if I go on a long vacation when I start showing?"

"Then what?" Faith grabs the glass of red wine from Brian. "Are you going to tell them you randomly found a newborn?"

"She might be going somewhere with this," Brian says. "Go to Bermuda and bring them another grandchild as a souvenir."

I use both hands to flip each one of them off.

"What about you get a boyfriend and have him become the baby daddy?" Faith suggests.

"Those few sips of wine must've hit you hard if you think I can just date someone, and he'll step up as the father. Who wants to date a fat, randomly knocked-up woman?"

Faith swirls a strand of her hair—the same color as mine—around her finger, deep in thought. "You could always rent a baby daddy."

"Rent a what?" I stutter.

"Have a guy pretend to be the dad for the time being, introduce him to Mom and Dad, and then say you broke up," she explains as if it were the most logical advice she'd ever given.

I scrunch my nose. "You're out of your mind."

"Am I, though?" She empties her glass, pours herself another, and opens the fridge.

"Funny," I grumble when she pulls out a juice box and slides it to me.

She smiles. "Think about it."

———

"HEY, BABE," Cassidy says when I enter our living room.

She and Lincoln are snuggled on the couch. *Schitt's Creek* is playing on the TV—most likely an episode we've seen twenty times. Two empty wineglasses, an empty pizza box, and a bag of Doritos are on the coffee table.

*Why does it seem like everyone is drinking when I can't?*

Jamie owns the two-bedroom townhome. After she moved in with Cohen, Georgia and I rented it from her. Not too long later, Georgia and Archer got their heads out of their butts and finally started dating. As much as I was happy for her, I was devastated when she broke the news of them living together. She promised not to move out until I found another roommate, knowing I'd rather burn my earlobes off than live alone.

Luckily, Cassidy overheard us talking about it and offered to move in. She lived alone in a small apartment, and like me, she didn't like being alone. A new fear surfaced of losing another roommate when she and Lincoln started dating. Even though they could stay in Archer's empty penthouse, they chose to stay here, so I wouldn't have to live by myself.

As great as it is, having them here, another worry has hit me since finding out about the pregnancy. Cassidy might've said she was okay with being in the next room over and helping with the baby, but eventually, when she's up all night, listening to the baby crying, she might change her mind and leave.

She pauses the show, sits up, and snags the Doritos. "How'd it go with your sister? Did you break the baby news?"

I nod, dropping my bag to the floor, and relax on the bright red chair across from them.

"What'd she say?" She chomps on a chip.

I blow out an upward breath. "Her genius advice was to rent a baby daddy."

Lincoln snorts, sweeping Cassidy's blonde hair off her shoulder before draping his arm over it. "That might be a lucrative business actually."

My shoulders slump. "Yes, but I can't afford to rent a baby daddy for eighteen years."

Cassidy licks cheese off her fingers. "Hopefully, you'll find someone to be a great dad by that time."

"I have a good idea," Lincoln says, kicking his feet onto the table. "What about Finn?"

I blankly stare at him. "What about him?"

"Have him be the baby daddy," Lincoln explains.

*I wish.*

I'd do anything for Finn to be the father instead of Gavin.

Cassidy perks up. "That's actually a really good idea." She kisses Lincoln's cheek. "Look at you, being all smart, baby."

Lincoln smiles with pride before smacking a kiss against Cassidy's lips.

I shake my head. "I can't ask him to do that."

"Why?" Cassidy asks. "I bet you twenty bucks he'd totally say yes."

# CHAPTER EIGHT

## Finn

NOT MUCH RELAXES ME.

I play the role of the opposite—the laid-back guy who cracks jokes and doesn't have a care in the world. I'm a good pretender —always have been. I tricked my teachers into thinking my dad worked so much that he wasn't able to attend any conferences or events. I convinced child services that I didn't stay home alone all night because my father was out, not giving a shit about his son.

I'm a survivor, and what better way to survive than to act like you don't give a shit?

At least tonight, being with friends will clear my mind from my dad's bullshit. The day after I paid for his car repairs, he called and needed money for his electric bill. He claimed it had to be paid in two hours or they'd shut it off.

It's his normal MO. He asks for shit last minute to create urgency of getting what he wants. You can't say, *Let me call you back in a few hours*, or question him because if you wait too long, there's always the dreaded reconnection fee.

Reconnection fees have fucked me more than any ex-girlfriend.

Like the dumbass I always am, I paid it while he bitched in the background on how dare I lecture where he spends his money.

"Less on drugs, more on bills," is what I'd said.

Only the guys know about my father, and out of respect for me, they've always kept it hush-hush around others. Grace discovering the trash I grew up as terrifies me. Her family is structured—wealthy and stand-up people. Not only that, but if her father has a good memory, he'd warn her about me.

It's the main reason that has stopped me from making her mine. There's too much against us to make it work, and now, her being pregnant with another man's baby only adds fuel to that messy fire.

The gang is already there when I walk into Cohen's back-yard. Our group tends to get together as often as we can. Cohen has a kick-ass yard, where we grill out, play cornhole, and celebrate special occasions if the weather isn't shitty.

As if on autopilot, I immediately scan the yard for Grace. I don't care what the occasion is; Grace is always the first person on my mind. She's sitting at a table with Georgia, Lola, Cassidy, Lincoln, and Silas, and before I reach them, I pause and smile, watching her from across the yard.

My favorite is when she doesn't know I'm watching or that she's on display for anyone. Laid-back Grace is the best Grace. It's a heavenly sight when she puts her guard down. Her playful behavior tears through that daily polished appearance. Just like my bliss is when I'm with our friends, it's also when the true Grace shines.

Her strawberry-blonde hair is pulled back from her face with two thick braids entwined along her forehead. Her plump lips are a soft pink, and a white silk top falls off one shoulder. Looking at Grace, you'd see her fitting into a puzzle with a man sporting loafers and a thousand-dollar polo. Not me—a man who doesn't give a shit what the label on his shirt says, who has a few tats and overgrown stubble on his cheeks.

We're not supposed to fit.

Yet we perfectly click.

For a moment, I forget how shit has changed for us, how we'll never be the same even though I'd pay for our friendship to never change course.

When her eyes meet mine, I stroll toward her.

A light brush of wind hits my cheeks when I stop behind her chair.

"Hey you," I say, wrapping my arms around her shoulders.

Her body relaxes against my touch, and a smile tugs at her lips when she tips her head back to peer at me. "Hi."

I give her shoulders a slight squeeze before pulling back and taking the chair next to her. It's open as if everyone knew next to her is always my spot.

I clasp my hands together and focus on her. "How are you feeling?"

She sighs. "I'm feeling okay ... just working and silently asking God why he made wine bad for pregnant women." Her cheeks turn rosy as she scrunches up her face. "Why can't wine be like vitamins? A daily prenatal glass of wine."

I chuckle before tipping my head toward Silas. "Make Grace a kick-ass nonalcoholic drink."

Silas isn't a drinker, so he's mastered the skill of concocting nonalcoholic drinks some would prefer over the real thing.

"I've already tried. Her pregnant taste buds think all of them suck," Silas replies, shrugging.

"I'm picky," Grace mutters.

My attention returns to her. "Other than the no-liquor inconvenience, how are *you* doing?"

"Shitty," Lincoln answers for her, bringing it to my attention that everyone's eyes are on us. "She needs a baby daddy. Any suggestions on where she can get one?"

"Seriously?" Grace narrows her eyes at him.

My gut twists, and I hate him for even mentioning that idea. "I can't help with that, babe, but if there's anything else you need—"

"You can help with it," Cassidy interrupts, leaning forward from across the table. "Do you have plans for the next six or seven months?"

I raise a brow, knowing where she's going with this but hoping I'm wrong.

Cassidy gestures to Grace, who's giving her a *shut up* signal by slicing her hand against her throat. "She needs a baby daddy, and, Finn, I think you're the man for the job."

"Don't listen to them," Grace rushes out. "They've been lucky enough to have alcohol, and they have lost their senses."

"Come on, Finn," Georgia cuts in. "Grace is nervous about telling her parents she's pregnant on top of there being no father. She hates disappointing people. I'd paint a beard on myself and stuff some socks into my pants to make it appear like I had a cock, but they already know me."

Grace does a sweeping gesture toward everyone at the table. "I am killing all of you."

"Look," Lincoln says, his eyes on me, "it's not like you have anything better to do. Everyone is coupled up, except Silas and you, and I doubt Grace wants Silas playing baby daddy."

Silas slaps his hand over his heart. "That's rude, asshole."

Lincoln shrugs. "It'll be a little awkward when you later become Lola's baby daddy."

Silas smirks at Lola, grabbing her chair and dragging it closer to his. "I'll take that."

Lola ruffles her hand through his thick hair. "In your dreams."

"Every damn night, baby." Silas slaps a kiss to her cheek, only inches from her lips.

"Back to the topic at hand," Cassidy says, her tone serious. "You game to play baby daddy, Finn?"

"You don't have to listen to them." Grace's voice is panicked.

"You should definitely listen to us," Georgia corrects.

All eyes are on me.

Everyone is quiet.

Including Grace.

As I peek at her, I read every emotion on her face.

There's fear.

I'm not sure which is stronger, though—fear of me rejecting the idea or fear of disappointing her family, who mean the world to her. She's not begging me to say no, not walking away, only staring ahead and waiting for my response.

"All right." I grab Lincoln's beer and chug it. "Why not?"

# CHAPTER NINE

## GRACE

# *Grace*

*"WHY NOT?"*

The words replay through my brain as if stuck.

*Did Finn just agree to ... play my baby daddy?*

*Pretty much said challenge accepted to our friends?*

Excitement buzzes through the air, our friends ecstatic over Finn agreeing to their crazy idea. Their elation and throwing out ideas of creating the perfect relationship deflect attention away from me—thank God. It gives me time to process the situation.

I refuse to peek at Finn, but I feel his stare pinned on me, searching for my reaction. Rather than ask me questions, Finn captures my hand and links our fingers together. He settles them on his knee—a silent reminder, assuring me that everything will be okay.

With perfect timing, Cohen interrupts the conversation.

"Food is ready!" he shouts, heading in our direction.

In one hand is a plate of burgers and steaks, and the other has hot dogs and chicken. Behind him, Jamie carries Isabella in her arms and Noah grips bags of chips.

Nausea curls at my stomach. Pulling away from Finn, I

cover my mouth, gagging, doing everything to hold in the urge to vomit.

Yet another reason to knee Gavin in the balls.

Not only do I get morning sickness, but certain foods also make me hurl.

Cohen places the plates on the table, and I can't stop myself from wincing and pushing back in my chair. The last thing I want to do is decorate tonight's dinner with my vomit.

Finn scoots in closer. "Everything okay?"

I gulp, another attempt to not puke, and shyly peek over at him. "The baby isn't a fan of meat."

He nods in understanding. "What is the baby a fan of?"

"Cupcakes ... deviled eggs ..." I scrunch up my nose in embarrassment. "Bagels dipped in taco sauce."

How I came up with that combo, I have no idea.

"That should be easy." He slaps his hand on the table and pulls himself to his feet. "I'll raid Cohen's kitchen, and if all else fails, we'll order something."

I grab his arm before gagging again, the wind pushing the odor toward me, making it stronger. "I don't want to be a pain. I'll hold my breath and snack on chips."

"Sorry, guys," Finn says, standing tall as if making an announcement. "I forgot to tell you, I'm trying the whole meat-less thing."

This time, I cover my mouth to mask a snort. Our friends' reactions are similar to mine. Finn's favorite meal is a juicy steak and veggies.

"Dude, you brought half the meat," Lincoln says.

"It was my turn to bring it," Finn says. "I'm not going to try to push my new lifestyle onto you."

Silas shrugs, suspiciously eyeing Finn before lifting his chin in his direction. "More for me then. Now, let's eat up."

"Feel free to raid the pantry," Jamie says while Cohen pulls out a chair and motions for her to sit.

"Thanks," he says, giving her a thumbs-up. He runs a finger along my arm, and I shiver. "Grace, I need some help."

Resting his palm against the base of my back, he veers me toward the house.

"Thank you for the save," I whisper, bumping my shoulder against his. Once again, he's saving my ass.

He bumps me back. "You know I always got your back, Mitchell."

It's a short walk to the back door, and we head into the kitchen. My heart thrashes into my chest now that we're alone and I'm no longer consumed with trying not to puke. Us being alone most likely means one of us will broach the subject of what he agreed to do.

He turns, resting his back against the fridge, and crosses his arms. "I figured you needed a minute ... and also that you didn't want to barf on everyone."

I shuffle my sandals along the floor. "I wasn't expecting that."

"That makes two of us, but given our friends, it shouldn't be much of a surprise."

"You don't have to do it, you know?"

Our friends can be pushy, and he was put on the spot.

If Finn fakes being my baby daddy, that'll momentarily stop him from dating someone else.

"Grace, look at me." His tone is stern.

I slowly lift my chin, our gazes meeting. Mine is giving off a *scared shitless* vibe. His is intense and concerned.

"Will it help you?"

I slowly nod. "It will."

"Then I'm game. Whatever you need, I'm here." He pauses to hold up a finger. "As long as you're okay with it. This is your decision, not our friends'."

"It's better than renting someone." I crack a forced smile.

"What?" He flinches. "You were going to *rent a dude*?"

"Negative. It was my sister's advice."

"Don't listen to your sister anymore. Whatever you need, I'm here." He pushes himself off the fridge. "Now, let's get you some *baby in your belly*–approved dinner."

---

TIMES I'VE BEEN JEALOUS:

1. Meeting one of Finn's flings.
2. Being ten and my mean cousin getting the Barbie Dreamhouse that I wanted from Santa.
3. Seeing Instagram models eat sixteen hot dogs and not gain a pound.

I rarely envy people, but at times, it sneaks up on me.

Today, it's snuck up on me like heartburn.

Sitting in my chair, I watch Finn play cornhole with Noah. They're on the same team—something not many adults like to do because they tend to lose when they're with the kid. But Finn? Finn never minds. He cheers Noah on every turn and high-fives him whether he misses or not.

A knot of regret forms in my gut, and the macaroni Finn made me earlier threatens to come up.

I wish I were pregnant with Finn's baby.

What I'd give for the role we'll soon be playing to be my reality.

Watching him, I know he'd be a better father than Gavin. I also love him, not Gavin. But it's too late for that now.

I'm used goods.

A woman pregnant by a married man.

"There you go!" Finn shouts after Noah throws the sack into the hole, lifting him up in the air.

Noah bursts into a fit of laughter.

That right there is a man I imagined being pregnant with.

Someone who doesn't mind forgoing their favorite meal to have boxed mac and cheese with me. A man who doesn't mind losing as long as a kid is happy.

Finn might tell people he doesn't deserve a woman like me, but he's wrong.

I don't deserve a man like him.

---

I WAKE up in a pool of sweat, every muscle in my body tight.

I'm in bed but in a state of terror and unaware of my surroundings. My heart pummels against my chest so hard that I wait for it to burst from my body.

I dart up from my bed, pushing my back against the headboard, and pull my knees to my chest. My hair is soaked, and I swat it away from my eyes as tears fall down my cheeks. Sucking in deep breaths, I attempt to calm myself, to stay quiet so I don't wake anyone.

It's been a while since I've had a nightmare ... especially one as realistic as the one I just had. They tend to make appearances when I'm stressed, feeling lost, struggling to cope with my reality.

What's more stressful than being knocked up by a man you can't stand?

My nightstand lamp shines next to me—a dim light so I'm still able to sleep at night—and I rock back and forth as if I were preparing to cradle the baby I'll soon have.

"Breathe in, breathe out," I repeat between sobs.

My lungs only knock harder against my chest, my breathing more panicked, the fear of suffocation rising through me. With shaking hands, I snatch my phone from my nightstand so hard that the charger falls off the wall.

I bite back a scream while calling Faith and cry her name into the phone when she answers.

"Another one?" Her voice is sleepy yet alert at the same time.

"Another one," I sob.

"Stay on the phone with me until you calm down, okay?"

I love my sister. There will never be another person who understands this bad side of me, this fear that is stuck to my core and will never be released, a flaw so deep that it's with me forever.

She stays with me on the phone—some time spent talking, some crying, and some in silence.

I don't hang up.

She waits until I'm sleeping to end the call.

# CHAPTER TEN

## *Finn*

"THERE'S THE BABY DADDY!" Silas shouts, his hand cupped over his mouth when I walk into Twisted Fox.

I flip him off while joining him at the pub table. "Real funny, asshole."

"You really doing this?" He stares at me with humor on his face.

I gulp. "I think so."

I haven't talked with Grace much since the whole *agreeing to be the fake baby daddy* thing. We didn't have much privacy at Cohen's. Last night, I texted and asked what she needed of me. Tomorrow, my role as her baby daddy will start, and I'm scared shitless.

Silas plants his elbow on the table and stares at me. "How do you feel about it?"

I suck in a breath. "It'll be ... weird."

"Nah, you and Grace are practically dating anyway." He snatches a fry from his red basket of food and tosses it into his mouth. "It won't be any different."

"Except I'm meeting her family ... her father, the *judge*."

"Oh fuck, I forgot about that."

At times, I forget who Grace's dad is, too, but then randomly, it'll creep back up—my past surfacing through the stained cracks. It's a reminder that no matter what, I'll always be my father's son. I was once on the same path as the man who puts me through the wringer daily. Not the drug part, but the *not getting my shit together and thinking rules don't apply to me* part. Thank God I dragged myself out of that life. That doesn't mean I haven't made mistakes that have come back to bite me in the ass.

"It's not like I can go back on my word now."

"Dude, I doubt he'll even remember you." He gestures to his basket. "A fry for your thoughts?"

I shake my head, my stomach roiling. "Let's hope he doesn't remember me."

I'm tight with all the guys in our circle, but Silas and I are the closest. Especially lately with everyone else being coupled up. We're two single guys who act like we're dating women we aren't.

We both have our secrets.

Shady pasts we've kept from people so they don't look at us differently.

"Want to do something tomorrow?" He pushes his basket up the table. "Watch the game? Have beers? Whatever to get you prepared for your new role?"

"Can't." I snatch up a fry. "Baby-daddy duties start tomorrow."

He smirks. "Which is?"

"Meeting the sister."

---

I DID some crazy shit in my early teens.

Blame it on lack of parental guidance.

Hating the world.

Rebelling as much as I could.

Not that I ever got in trouble.

There was no grounding for me because that would have meant my father would have to parent—something John Duke had no time for.

But what I'm doing with Grace?

It takes the cake.

I wipe my sweaty hands down my jeans as I walk up her porch stairs and knock on the front door. It swings open, and Grace stands in front of me. A worried smile stains her pink lips as she nervously waves me inside. As soon as she shuts the door behind me, I pull her into a tight hug—an assurance that everything will go smoothly today.

"Day one of us fake dating and acting like I knocked you up," I say, cracking a smile as we pull away.

She slowly nods. "At least I don't have to lie yet since my sister already knows we're faking."

I bite into my tongue, holding back from saying, *What if we don't fake it?*

If someone were to ask me what my dream life was, it wouldn't be riches, mansions, or an endless supply of women. It'd be a life with Grace—her in my bed, wearing the diamond ring I picked out, and having our children.

I do a sweeping gesture down her body. "I'd like to throw out that my fake baby mama looks hot as hell today."

No matter what Grace wears, she always looks fucking adorable. Her style changes from day to day, but she usually sports loose-fitting dresses or casual clothes when it's just our friends and us. Today, she's chosen a yellow sundress that hangs loose off one shoulder and ends inches from her ankles, showing off glittery sandals. Her hair is in another crown braid —her signature style—and the only makeup she's wearing is a light-pink shimmer over her eyes.

She blushes. "You clean up pretty well yourself."

I dragged Silas and Lola out shopping this morning to help me dress the part of Grace's boyfriend. My usual casual tee has been traded out for a black collared button-down. Grace only brought a few guys around us before we became close, and none of them resembled me. Not that I want to look like them either.

You can bet your ass, you'll never catch me sporting khaki shorts with creases in the middle and a sweater draped over my neck.

*No fucking thank you.*

A moment of awkwardness passes—something that hasn't happened in our relationship in years but seems to have become the regular since her pregnancy news broke.

I study her for a moment, double-checking she's not too stressed, and I check my watch. "You ready to go?"

She nods. "As ready as I'll ever be."

Leaving the house, I guide her to my Challenger, open the passenger door, and wait until she slides in before joining her.

During the drive, my mind scrambles.

*How will we end this game?*

*When will we know it's time to pull the plug?*

*How deep will it wound our relationship when we stop playing pretend?*

It's too late to back out now.

———

I SHIFT my car into park and turn in my seat to peer at Grace. "You nervous?"

Hell, my nerves might be climbing higher than hers.

It's not every day you fake being a woman's baby daddy—especially when you wish it were true.

I'd do anything for this woman to be mine, but I was too chickenshit to take my shot.

"A little," she replies, fidgeting with a charm on her bracelet.

"How strong will the interrogation be?"

"My sister is nice but can be overprotective." She unbuckles her seat belt. "Now's your chance to back out. Speak now or forever hold your peace."

"No backing out, babe. I'm here for as long as you need me."

Her shoulders relax. "You're too good to me."

*No, you're too good for me.*

I reach over my console and capture her hand in mine, running my finger along her soft skin. "We got this, babe. We've made a badass team for years. It was about time we stepped our game up to see what else we could do."

She repeatedly nods as if my pep talk is convincing her. "You're right. We got this."

I kiss the top of her hand before releasing her and cut the engine.

Grace's sister's neighborhood is exactly what I expected. A gated entrance; a large, grassy lawn, manicured to perfection; and a home that could be featured in a magazine.

It's a far cry from where I came from.

I wasn't the rich kid in school.

I wasn't even the middle-class kid.

I was the dirt-poor boy whose hand-me-downs stank of cigarette smoke and whose father showed up to one of my football games, drunk off his ass, demanding I give him money for *all the shit he's done for me.* Rich kids mocked me until they realized I'd beat their asses. After a few punches to their faces, the jerks' shit-talking lessened. That didn't mean they still didn't look down on me.

Facial expressions always speak louder than words.

Grace adjusts her dress, inhales a steady breath, and steps out of the car. I do the same and am by her side. The scent of fresh-cut grass follows us up the driveway to the bright red front door surrounded by potted plants.

Without bothering to knock, Grace walks us in.

"Hello," she calls out while entering the expansive entryway.

There's shiplap—shiplap everywhere.

I only know what damn shiplap is because Grace and Georgia used to force me to watch some HGTV shit, and every damn homeowner wanted their walls covered in the shit.

Apparently, Grace's sister fits that bill as well.

"In the kitchen!" someone out of view yells.

My attention shifts to the stairs as Raven, Grace's niece, comes barreling down the stairs.

"Aunt Grace!" she yells, stomping down each step. "You brought Finn! He's my friend!"

Raven tags along with Grace sometimes, especially when Noah is involved. They've become good friends, and it gives Noah someone to play with. During our last trip to a ski lodge for Noah's birthday, she told me she asks her parents for a little brother or sister daily. I'm sure having a cousin will help too.

I grin. "I sure am."

I'm good with kids—at least, that's what people tell me. Hell, half the time, I'd rather sit and chat with a kiddo than an adult.

Raven's red-hued pigtails bounce in the air as she hops on her feet. "Maybe we can play games later?"

"Maybe." Grace plays with her braid, twirling it around her fingers.

Grace squeezes Raven's shoulder. "Let's see what your mom is up to."

"Oh, she's just making dinner," Raven says, throwing her hand up as if it were no big deal while we meander down a hallway. "She's making me dino nuggets, though, because it's what I want."

Grace laughs. "You're going to end up turning into a dino nugget."

"Hey now," I say, winking at Raven. "Dino nuggets are pretty darn good."

She squeals, clapping her hands, her walk turning into a skip. "See, Mommy! Finn loves dino nuggets too!"

Reaching the kitchen, we stop. The smell of garlic smacks me in the face as I do a quick once-over of my surroundings. It's a big-ass kitchen with more shiplap, stainless steel appliances, and baby-blue cabinets. It's a kitchen you'd normally find in a farmhouse, not a home like this.

"Hey, guys!"

My gaze shifts to the island, where a spitting image of Grace stands—only taller and with more blond in her hair. She smiles at us while slicing a knife through a tomato on the cutting board.

Grace steps to my side, somewhat in front of me as if she were my bodyguard. "Finn, this is my sister, Faith."

With the knife still in her hand, Faith waves at me, tomato juice slipping onto the counter. "Hi, Finn." She shoots a mischievous look to Grace. "We've heard so much about you. You sounded too good to be true, so Brian and I had a bet that you weren't real."

"Really?" Grace grumbles with a scowl.

"He's real, Mommy!" Raven jumps up and down and points at me. "He buys me ice cream too!"

"Yes, she always raves about the ice cream you get her," a guy says, walking into the kitchen, holding a bottle of wine. "Can I get you something to drink, Finn? A juice box for you, Grace?"

Grace rolls her eyes. "You should really go on the road since your jokes are so original. I'm sure no pregnant girl has heard that one before." She motions toward the guy. "This is my brother-in-law, Brian."

The guy dramatically bows. "Thank you. I always knew you appreciated my jokes."

I expected something different—snobbery or an upturned nose—but these people seem as laid-back as our friends.

Sure, the size of their home, the large rock on Faith's finger, and the expensive bottle of wine Brian is opening scream money, but their personalities scream cool.

"Beer?" Brian asks. "Jack and Diet? We have a full bar, so anything you want, I can grab you."

"I'll have a water." I don't want Grace to feel like the odd one out of drinking.

"I'll take one of those juice boxes ..." Grace pauses. "Actually, why don't you grab the juicer and make me some fresh OJ, Brian?"

"Why don't you drink Raven's sugar-free shit?" He smirks.

"Daddy said a bad word!" Raven says with a scowl.

"Finn, I hope eggplant parmigiana is okay with you," Faith says. "Meat makes Grace sick, so we're trying an alternative."

Grace pulls out a stool under the island, and I grab her hand, helping her jump up onto it.

Gripping the back of the stool, I reply, "That's fine with me."

And now, we get ready for our baby daddy game to start.

# CHAPTER ELEVEN

# Grace

"I LIKE HIM," Faith says when we're alone. "Like, really like him and could totally smack you for not getting knocked up by him." She shoves my shoulder. "I swear, for someone who's so damn smart, you fail in the dating department."

We're outside on the patio after dinner. We ate outside, and the fresh air helped calm my nerves. No one brought up the game Finn and I are playing. Most likely because Raven was with us, and that girl is the definition of the game Telephone. Never say anything in front of her you don't want our entire family to find out about.

Finn had to take a phone call, and Brian left to grab Faith another glass of wine.

I lean in closer, lowering my voice in case Finn comes back. "We are *friends*. That's it."

"Mm-hmm." Sarcasm coats her tone.

I don't know why I was nervous about Finn meeting Faith and Brian. They get along with nearly everyone. While I helped Faith with dinner, Finn and Brian made small talk. It was comfortable, and I wish I hadn't realized I could've had this sooner before getting involved with Gavin. We could've had this if we weren't too terrified of commitment with each other.

Gavin has never met my family.

I've never met his ... for obvious reasons I now know.

Now, after discovering the real Gavin, I know Faith would've probably hated him.

It's different with Finn—the stakes are higher.

We're not just friends anymore.

Us playing pretend will create more attachment to each other.

It's a dangerous game we're playing—the game of *everything we've ever wanted.*

And no doubt, our feelings will grow as this plays out. I'll discover what it's like to be his girlfriend, but eventually, he'll pull away at the end, and I'll be left broken. I need to start preparing myself for when that day comes.

"Now, it's planning time," Faith says, snapping me out of my thoughts.

I raise a brow. "What do you mean?"

She flips her long hair over her slender shoulder. "Mom and Dad will ask questions—*lots* of them. They'll drill you on every detail, so you need to be prepared. You and Finn need to be on the same page—how you met, how you got pregnant—"

"That one is fairly obvious," I interrupt.

She swats my shoulder. "You know what I mean. They'll ask Finn how he plans to support you and the baby, if he's ready to become a father, why he didn't pop the question before knocking you up—all that personal shit."

The thought of my father's interrogation sends a chill up my spine.

"Jesus," I hiss. "Did they cross-examine Brian like that?"

She shakes her head. "Brian and I were married, though. Dad had already interrogated him when we started dating. Our pregnancy wasn't a shocker ... wasn't with a man they'd never even heard of." She levels her eyes on me, her expression turning stern. "Therefore, tie those loose ends before they unravel in front of Mom and Dad."

"I guess we'll"—I scrunch up my nose—"tie stuff up."

I haven't even planned on when I'm telling my parents, and I'm already stressed.

I have to train myself on being a better liar before I enter that rabbit hole.

"You need a clear, concise plan," Faith continues. "That starts with you moving in together."

I picked the perfect time to take a sip of water and spit it out at her words. "Excuse me?"

Her face is serious. "You are dating, having a baby, but not living together? That screams suspicious."

"I'll blame it on them not wanting me to move in with a guy before marriage."

"You're knocked up. They'll at least expect that."

"Easier said than done. I live in a two-bedroom and have a roommate I can't exactly kick out."

"Share a room with Finn then." She throws out the suggestion so casually as if it were sharing ice cream, not a bed.

"You've had too much wine." I snatch her glass and set it out of her reach. "You're cut off."

She stands up from her chair enough to confiscate her glass from me. "Think about it, okay?" She chugs it. "It'll make your story much more believable. Mom and Dad will believe the relationship is serious and that you didn't get knocked up by some rando."

She makes a point there.

My parents will immediately think Finn and I aren't serious if we're living separately and we haven't met each other's parents, therefore not taking our *relationship* to the next level.

"We'll lie about living together." My mouth grows dry at the thought of another lie, and I wish I could yell for Brian to pour me a glass too. "There. Problem solved."

"You're racking up the lies there, dear sister." She shifts in her chair, relaxing against the back. "On another note, while you're hiding from Mom and Dad, where are you going to crash when Lincoln and Cassidy work at night? You either need to come clean to them soon, sleep here, or be alone." All playfulness in her tone has vanished. "If they find out Finn works late nights at the bar, they won't believe you live together. They know you'd never be with someone who couldn't be with you at night."

*Crap.*

She has a point.

A big freaking point.

I thought I was figuring it out, and then she had to throw a wrench in that plan.

"He works at night, and I can't ask him to quit his job," I say, my voice strained. I grip the arms of my chair. "Not to mention, I can't ask my roommates to move out."

She stares at me intently. "You said before that Lincoln and Cassidy have another place, but they haven't moved out because they don't want to bail on you. Can you ask them to stay there until you get stuff figured out? You also need to talk to them about plans for when you have the baby. Will the baby sleep in your room?"

"I hate when you ask all the questions," I grumble.

"That's what a big sister is for." She brushes her hand along my arm. "Look, everything will be okay."

"All right, sorry about that," Finn says, strolling toward us and sliding his phone into his pocket.

He arrives at the same time Brian returns with a beer in one hand.

I offer Finn a smile that fails to reach my eyes. "Totally fine."

Faith locks her fingers together and rests them on the table. "Finn, how do you feel about moving in with Grace?"

Finn stops mid-step.

# CHAPTER TWELVE

## Finn

THERE WERE things I expected from meeting Grace's sister.

Questions regarding my job.

Asking if I was good at faking being someone's boyfriend.

What I'd do when the charade was over.

None of those questions came to the surface.

What I got instead was ...

*"How do you feel about moving in with Grace?"*

Faith said it casually as if she asked me if I wanted dessert.

"What?" I stutter, my mouth dropping open.

The idea never occurred to me. I assumed Grace and I were only playing our game around her parents, but moving in together? That makes it more real. It'd be more than faking it. We'd be *living* it.

All eyes are on me.

Grace's panicked.

Faith's in expectation.

Brian's unsurprised.

"You don't ... you don't have to do that," Grace rushes out. "As you can see, my sister loves wine, and it's made her come up with crazy ideas."

Faith holds up a finger. "Your first statement is true. The second isn't crazy." She waves her hands toward the table. "Take a few breaths. I'm sure my question was a shocker, but now, let's talk about it."

"Okay," I drawl out. "Let's, uh ... talk about it."

"You don't have to do this," Grace says as soon as I sit back down.

"Our parents will expect you to be living together," Faith says, and I'm figuring out now why she became an attorney. "It's something they'll expect. If you're not married, it'd at least show that there's a commitment somewhere."

"This is all new to us," I croak. "We're pretty much playing it as we go."

My head scrambles.

*Could I do that?*

*Live with her and not want her more?*

*Play house before jumping ship and acting like it never happened?*

"Are you going to keep working at Twisted Fox?" Faith asks, clearly in charge of the conversation.

"Jesus, Faith." Grace releases an exasperated breath. "The only interrogation Finn expects is from our parents, not you."

Faith shakes her head. "Mom and Dad will never believe you're dating if he's not there with you at night."

Grace's face pales. "Finn can't exactly move his work schedule around. People don't go barhopping in the morning."

"What if you had another job, Finn?" Brian asks, looking me straight in the eye.

I hold his eye contact. "What do you mean?"

He leans back in his chair, gripping the neck of his beer. "You can work at Luxury Imports."

Luxury Imports is a chain of dealerships that specializes in selling high-end and hard-to-find luxury cars. You nearly need a black card to test-drive a car there. I've never been inside, but

Archer purchased his car from them. Pretty sure Lincoln did too.

I bend my neck forward to hide the shock on my face. "Man, I can't ask you to do that."

"You didn't ask. I offered." There's no hesitation in Brian's tone—no, *my wife is making me do this.* No, the dude is genuinely offering me a job at one of the largest chains of car dealerships in the state.

As much as I'd love to take the offer, I can't.

"My best friends own the bar I work in," I say, raising my chin. "I can't up and leave them."

"What about working at the bar only a few nights a week and supplementing that income by working at my place? I have a few different positions that I think you'd be perfect for." He smiles. "Your pick."

Silence passes over the table.

"How about this?" Brian finally says, knocking his knuckles against the table. "I'll pay double what you make at the bar, and you won't have to work nights. You'll get benefits, a 401(k), all that good stuff. I know you don't want to let your friends down, but this is a great opportunity for you."

I hide my shaking hands under the table. "What about when Grace and I break off"—I refuse to glance at her—"whatever this is?"

Brian sits up straight. "You'll still have a job for as long as you like. I think you'll be a good fit. Trust me, I wouldn't have offered if I'd thought you'd be a shit employee."

———

GRACE'S VOICE is frantic as soon as we get into my car. "Don't feel obligated to take that job, Finn. I know tonight was a lot, and I hadn't planned on any of that going down. I'd figured they'd have questions, but I had no idea. I swear, I had no part in it."

I place my hand over her trembling one.

"Are you mad?" she asks at my silence.

I sag against the seat. "I didn't earn it."

I don't like favors.

They always come with a price, an *I did this for you.*

Blame it on a father who throws every damn thing in your face—*I made sure you were fed, I bought you clothes to cover your back, I gave you a roof to sleep under.* Every time my father did me a favor, it was thrown in my face.

That's why I never ask for help.

Why, sometimes, my pride bites me in the ass.

"Finn," Grace says, her voice softening, "sometimes opportunities come as luck. You're putting your life on hold for me. You deserve this. You've earned it. It's not easy to land a job at Luxury Imports. It's not your typical car dealership. It's a big deal."

"And what about the *moving in with you* thing?"

# CHAPTER THIRTEEN

# Grace

SILENCE IS in the air while Finn walks me to my front door.

I turn to look at him and fiddle with the keys in my hand. "Cass and Lincoln are home. Unless you want to be interrogated by them next, I wouldn't suggest you come in."

We only spent a few hours at Faith's, but Finn appears as if he's been through the wringer.

It's the same with me.

Topics came up that I hadn't expected.

My life has become a spinning wheel of answers to endless questions.

He scratches his cheek. "Text me later?"

I nod. "Thank you so much for doing this, Finn. It means a lot."

"Grace, anything you need, I'm here. Good night."

He pecks a kiss to my forehead and waits for me to walk inside before returning to his car. As I drop my keys on the entry table, thoughts of how much my life is changing hit me.

I enter the living room to find Cassidy and Lincoln on the couch, snuggled as usual and watching TV. Our living room is where we spend most of our free time. Cassidy and Lincoln are homebodies, like me. We binge-watch shows, eat junk food, and have our friends over for game nights. It's on the smaller side, but the open floor plan is great for entertaining.

Cassidy raises her head from Lincoln's chest and sits up. "How'd it go, babe?"

Collapsing onto a chair, I rub my forehead. "I'm done with questions for tonight ... or heck, even the next year."

She laughs. "All right, I'll wait until the morning to drill you on how well Finn played the boyfriend role."

"Not only did they tell him to move in with me but they also want him to work for Luxury Imports."

Cassidy and Lincoln stay quiet, staring while waiting for an explanation.

I give them what they want. "They think it'll be more believable to my parents."

"What did Finn say?" Lincoln asks, stroking his jaw.

"He's hesitant about the job because he doesn't want to bail on Cohen and Archer after he's worked for them for so long." I stop myself from slapping a hand over my mouth.

Archer is Lincoln's brother, and I'd feel terrible if he told Archer about Finn's job offer before Finn had a chance to talk to him. I gulp before remembering this is Lincoln, and he's one of the most trustworthy people I know.

"Is it better pay?" Cassidy asks.

I nod.

Lincoln settles his gaze on me. "I guarantee you, if Finn tells them it's a better opportunity, they'll be happy for him."

He's right. Our circle of friends is supportive of each other, no matter what. We will step up and do anything to help because we're like family.

"I promise I'm not saying this to stress you out," Cassidy starts.

"You saying something isn't meant to stress me out will definitely stress me out," I interrupt.

She laughs. "Well then, prepare to be stressed for a minute." Her voice turns gentle as she stares at me. "What will you and Finn do after the baby is born ... after you're finished convincing your parents that he's the dad?"

I hate that question because I have no idea how to answer it.

*Will we stay friends?*

*Will we have a fake breakup plan?*

"I haven't thought that far ahead." I narrow my gaze on her. "You guys are the ones who came up with the genius plan. I guess you can come up with post-baby plans too."

"You two could"—Cassidy hesitates as if trying to come up with the right words—"stay together."

"Oh, come on," I sing out, dropping back my head.

"What?" She perks up. "I'm sure Finn would be okay with that plan."

A knot ties in my belly. "Have you seen the girls Finn has dated? They're the opposite of me. We're friends. That's it."

"No, I actually haven't," she replies. "In all the time that I've known Finn, I've never seen him with another woman other than you ... and our friends, of course."

The air starts to grow heavy.

My breathing grows ragged.

*She's right.*

Finn stopped bringing girls to our social gatherings years ago.

He doesn't entertain women who flirt with him at the bar, but I'm also not stupid. Just because he doesn't flirt with them in front of me doesn't mean he's abstained from sex. I find it as more of a respect thing for me.

"Same," Lincoln inputs, twirling a strand of Cassidy's blond hair around his finger. "Nor have I heard him even mention another woman."

"You two have sexual chemistry off the charts," Cassidy

adds, nodding with certainty. "Try it. What do you have to lose?"

"Um, our friendship," I say like *duh*.

"Cass and I were scared of that too," Lincoln says, shooting Cassidy a flirtatious grin. "When we got our heads out of our asses and took the risk, it was worth it." Throwing his arm around Cassidy's shoulders, he drags her closer to him and kisses the slant of her jaw. "It's what happened with all our friends. Take that damn risk, Grace. You only have one life, and trust me, shit can change in an instant." He snaps his fingers. "I know that from experience."

"I'll think about it."

Apprehension and fear gather within me. Lincoln and Cassidy take the hint that I've had enough talk, and our conversation gears toward a *drunken idiot at the bar* story. The conversation of Finn moving in doesn't arise again. I'm not sure if it's them giving me a mental break or if they're upset with me. I make a mental note to ask when my nerves aren't on fire.

It's not long until I tread down the hallway and into my bedroom. I pull my phone from my bag to find a good-night text from Finn.

As I slide into bed, my brain goes through memories of Finn.

Other than my father, he's been the most reliable man in my life. When he says he'll be there, he'll be there.

I trust Finn with my life ... but can I trust him with my heart?

# CHAPTER FOURTEEN

## *Finn*

MY EYES ARE heavy as I walk into Twisted Fox.

I spent my night thinking about Brian's job offer. I'd made it clear to everyone at dinner last night that I wouldn't make any decisions until I talked to my friends.

As soon as Cohen and Archer decided to open Twisted Fox, they offered me a job. I've worked in bars for as long as I've legally been able to.

Okay, that's a lie.

I *helped* in one before I was even legally able to get my license. My father was a frequent patron at a local bar, and since I was the one always picking him up, the owner hired me to pick up trash and miscellaneous bullshit while I was waiting on my dad to have *just one more*.

I think the owner felt sorry for me and didn't want me at home with no supervision that young. He paid me under the table. It wasn't much, but it paid for my food and the school supplies my father was too broke to buy me. It also paid for the times he held out his hand, asking for every penny I had to make my contribution to the bills.

When I turned twenty-one, I started legally working in bars

since it was quick money. It stuck, and I've stayed with it since. Working in bars is what led me to my friends, and I'll always be thankful for that.

Cohen is one of the kindest dudes I know. He's had it rough, practically raising his sister and then becoming a single dad. The baby mama dipped on him right after giving birth, and then years later, he started hanging out with her younger sister. Some drama happened, but now, they're happy.

I rub the back of my neck before knocking on Cohen's office door. The door is open, but he's my boss, so I respect his privacy and wait for him to let me in.

Cohen looks away from his phone and toward the doorway. "Hey, man."

I rock back on my heels. "Can I talk to you and Archer real quick?"

"Sure." His brows draw together as he sets his phone down and stands. "We'll go to his office because he'll bitch if he has to come to mine."

I chuckle. "Fact."

As much as we love Archer, the dude has to be the crankiest son of a bitch I've ever met—and I grew up around addicts. He's not a people person, but that doesn't mean he doesn't have a big heart.

We walk the few steps to Archer's office, and unlike Cohen's, the door is shut. There's never an open invitation into Archer's world.

"Just a minute," Georgia yells from the other side after I knock.

I cast a glance to Cohen, who's pulling at his hair.

"They're having relationship talks in there," he says.

I paste on a smile. "That's definitely what they're doing."

Neither of us is convinced that's what's happening behind Archer's closed door.

The door flies open, and Georgia walks out, straightening out her skirt.

"Really?" Cohen grumbles.

"What?" Georgia asks, her cheeks red. "We were discussing the schedule."

I snort.

Cohen motions toward the hallway. "Go home and read the Bible."

She smirks and waves good-bye.

Archer reclines in his chair, his large stature making the desk appear small. He eyes us suspiciously as if we're coming to him with a problem. He prefers to pour drinks and handle business, not deal with employee drama.

Cohen does a sweeping gesture of the room, pinching his lips together. "Dude, do whatever you want *under your own roof*. Not here."

Archer's mood is unreadable. "I expect the same rules to apply to you and Jamie then." A flicker of a self-satisfied smile briefly flashes along his lips.

Cohen flips him off.

"To what do I owe the pleasure?" Archer asks, getting straight to the point.

Cohen casts a glance my way.

"I was offered a job," I say before stopping and holding up a finger. "Not that I was looking. Grace's brother-in-law offered me a position at his company since I'll be there for the whole" —I hesitate, my mouth turning dry as I search for the right explanation—"pregnancy thing."

My attention moves back and forth between Archer and Cohen.

Cohen is the first to speak. "So, is this a full-time thing?" He raises a brow. "I thought it was playing pretend in front of her parents?"

I suck in a breath. "Honestly, I have no idea. Grace is having issues with the baby's father, and I don't want her to go through this alone. If she needs someone to help play dad for a minute, I'm game."

Cohen nods. "Understandable."

"That's how the job offer came to life," I tell them. "They want me to be with her at night since Cassidy and Lincoln sometimes work late."

"If it's a better opportunity for you, take it," Archer inputs. "If the job fucking sucks, you're welcome back here at any time. Don't feel obligated to stay here. I don't want to hold you back from a good thing."

"Agreed." Cohen slaps me on the back. "Congrats, man."

I smile. "Thank you."

"One question, though," Cohen says before I leave the room. "Do you have to wear a suit?"

Archer snorts. "Oh God, are you going to start wearing fucking loafers, Finn?"

This time, I'm the one flipping Archer off ... and then I direct it to Cohen. "Both of you, fuck off."

Cohen laughs. "We're going to miss you, and your ass had still better come hang out here."

"That'll never change."

---

I PULL the business card from my wallet and stare at it.

Never did I think I'd ever have a job opportunity like this.

I was born into a white-trash family, to addicts, to nothing but scum. They're all labels I've heard my entire life. At first, it hurt to hear the truth, but as time went on, I started agreeing with them.

*Meth addicts.*
*Thieves.*
*Deceitful.*

Those words described the few family members I knew of.

I dial the number, a hard swallow with each digit.

"Brian," I say when he answers, "it's Finn. Grace's—"

"I know who you are," Brian says with a deep chuckle, his voice matching the millionaires you see in business movies.

"I'll take the job." I say this with deep confidence, so he doesn't regret the offer.

That strong tone lowers. "Thank you."

*He's thanking me?*

I shake my head even though he can't see me. "No, thank you."

"It means a lot to Faith and me that we'll have someone there for Grace. When can you start?"

"Whenever you need me."

"Tomorrow?"

"Tomorrow works."

My life is changing more and more each day.

# CHAPTER FIFTEEN

## Finn

I'VE NEVER FELT SO out of place in my life.

Never felt like a damn poser.

It was a forty-five-minute drive to the dealership since no one in Anchor Ridge has the bank account to purchase a vehicle that costs as much as some people's homes. I felt poor as fuck as I parked in the parking lot filled with cars I'd never seen before.

As soon as I walked into the dealership this morning, my surroundings screamed wealth. Every wall was made of shiny glass. Range Rovers, Bentleys, a Lamborghini, and Mercedes decorated the showroom floor. There was an entire bar with expensive waters, champagne, and snacks in the corner. Nothing like I'd ever witnessed.

Brian greeted me, his bright smile wide, to give me a tour and go through all my employee shit. My mouth dropped open when he disclosed not only my pay but also the commission I'd receive from selling these high-end cars.

From the whispers, I learned it was uncommon for the VP of the company to pay so much attention to a new employee who hadn't proven himself worthy of selling one car.

*"Whose dick did he suck to get this job?"*

*"Nepotism at its fucking finest. I'm sure it's a cousin, friend, sister's boyfriend. Dude isn't even wearing an expensive suit."*

All comments I heard in the background.

Unfortunately, unlike my job at Twisted Fox, I can't throw an asshole out for talking shit. This will take some adjusting.

At least Tim, the guy training me, is cool, but he caught on that Brian and I had a personal relationship. Unless he wanted to lose his job, he had to be nice to me.

Something else I'm not used to is early mornings. I chugged a coffee on my drive before chasing it with an energy drink and am still struggling to keep my eyes open. It didn't help that I had been awake until four this morning since I worked a shift last night.

What a dumbass move to tell him I could start today.

"All right, man," Tim said. "You ready to learn about some badass cars? Another perk of the job? We get to test-drive them."

---

"WANT TO GRAB LUNCH?" Brian asks, poking his head into Tim's office and interrupting him schooling me on the differences between Mercedes models. "Celebrate your new job?"

A rip of guilt presses through me as I shake my head. "I appreciate the offer, but I'm bringing Grace lunch."

I've never done that before since our sleeping schedules were opposite. But things have changed now, as we're not only friends, and I want to see her. The school she teaches at isn't far from here, and it'll be nice to surprise her.

I also need a break from the dealership, and no doubt if I have lunch with Brian, there will be work talk. Grace is always a breath of fresh air ... like a damn Prozac when I'm having a

hard time. She's an optimist, always seeing the glass as half-full
—the opposite of me.

We make a good team.

She keeps me positive.

I keep her from dealing with shitty situations by herself.

Not wanting to feel like a jackass, I add, "Tomorrow?"

He smiles and nods. "You did a good job today. Tim said
you're catching on well."

---

I TEXT Grace as soon as I get in my car.

**Me: Can I bring my baby mama some lunch?**

It's not until I hit send that I realize I didn't put *fake* in front
of *baby mama*.

It's the first time there's no reference to it being fake when it
comes to us dating or her being pregnant with "my" baby.

My phone beeps with a reply minutes later.

**Grace: I'd love that. Lunch break starts in 10.**

**Me: Craving anything specific?**

**Grace: Surprise me.**

**Me: Be there soon.**

I drive to her favorite bistro she likes when we're closer to
the city, order our sandwiches, and rush to my car. The faster I
get there, the more time I can spend with her before our breaks
get cut off. I pull into the school's parking lot, kill the engine,
and jump out of the car.

The sun peeks through the clouds, and I pass benches
spread along the walkway and rows of pine trees while heading
toward the brick building. Today isn't the first time I've been to
Sunset Hill. I came once when Grace was hosting a charity
auction and another time when she needed help bringing in
supplies for the new school year.

Light classical music plays when I enter the administration office.

"Hey there," a woman behind the desk greets, setting her coffee cup down. Her lips are dark red with a slight smudge on the corner.

"Hi," I reply, holding up the sandwich bag. "I'm here to visit Grace Mitchell."

I'm not sure if I should've said her full name or Miss Mitchell. Mitchell is a common name, and this isn't a student I'm talking to.

She grins, tapping her finger toward a clipboard on the desk. "Sign in here, please. I need your driver's license. We'll get you a name tag, sweetie." She picks up the phone. "Hey, Miss Mitchell. You have a guest here to see you." She wiggles her fingers in giddiness, and I automatically like her.

Setting the bag and drinks down, I jerk my wallet from my pants and hand her my license.

I grab the pencil to sign my name when I hear a harsh voice say, "Miss Mitchell, huh?"

I scribble my name down before looking up to find a man walking in my direction. His gaze is stony as he stands next to the secretary.

He scowls at me. "Are you her brother? Relative?"

I chuckle, offering an amused smile. There's nothing better than ruining a guy's attempt at being an asshole by not taking the bait. "Nah, definitely not her brother."

His back straightens. "What are you to her then?"

"Finn!" Georgia says, exiting a room and heading in our direction. She motions to the bag. "I hope you brought me something too."

Georgia is the school counselor at Sunset Hill.

"Shit, sorry," I reply, feeling like an asshole for forgetting her.

"Rude." Her voice is playful. "Next time, I'll be sure to text my order."

I salute her. "I got you."

The man clears his voice. "You never answered the question as to who you are."

Georgia moves in closer. The playfulness in her tone changes to disgust. "That's none of your business."

The secretary gapes at them.

"I'm the principal," the man grinds out. "Everything that happens here is my business."

Before anyone can throw out a response to this asshole, the door opens, and Grace walks in, looking her gorgeous self.

Grace is beautiful.

Period.

No exceptions.

She's gorgeous when she's dressed in her sexy-as-fuck teacher clothes.

When she's wearing loose clothes, overalls, or those long dresses she likes to wear.

When she's sporting sweats with a runny red nose, and I bring her chicken soup when she's sick.

She grins brightly. "Hey, Finn."

"A new friend?"

Her shoulders tighten, and her gaze swings to the man.

"An *old* friend," Georgia corrects snidely. "More than that actually."

Grace gestures to the guy. "Finn, this is Principal Long."

I lift my chin, and it kills me to say, "Nice to meet you, man."

I'm not sure how much power this dude has, but I plan on lunch visits with Grace to become a regular thing. I can't have him giving us a hard time.

"Pleasure." The snarl on his face confirms it's not.

I clench my jaw.

Grace is running her fingers through her hair.

Georgia is practically snarling at the man.

"We're having lunch," Grace tells Georgia, breaking the awkward tension. "Want to join us?"

She shakes her head. "Archer and I are having a Zoom lunch." She winks. "It appears we both have lunch dates."

"This isn't a place for dates," Principal Long scolds.

"Is that your boyfriend, Miss Mitchell?"

I spin on my heels to find a little girl sitting in the chair in the corner of the room. Her bright pink bookbag is settled on her lap, and she's sending a gap-toothed smile at Grace.

Everyone looks at Grace for an answer.

# CHAPTER SIXTEEN

# Grace

"IS THAT YOUR BOYFRIEND?"

Lizzy, the questioner, is the pigtailed girl in the corner, waiting on a parent to pick her up. She was my student last year and a nosy one. With Gavin's hostile questioning, I'm not sure if anyone noticed her.

Everyone is staring at me in expectation. All of them wanting me to share my personal life as if it were a job requirement. Georgia and Finn already know the situation. Rachelle, the secretary, who appeared lost during Gavin's questioning, shifts excitedly in her chair, awaiting her chance to share today's gossip in the teachers' lounge later. Gavin's grinding his teeth, and from the spiteful expression on his face, I'm positive he'll bug me about this later.

Deciding to ignore the question, I settle my attention on Finn. "We can eat in my room."

I'm done pleasing people with information.

Gavin is my superior, but I don't owe him any details of my personal life. He lost that privilege when I found out he was a married prick. Finn and I do need to chat about how we'll define our relationship to others.

I didn't expect Finn to bring me lunch, and I was giddy when I read his text.

Gavin clicks his tongue against the roof of his mouth. "We don't recommend guests for lunch. Next time, I suggest you make dinner plans."

Unsure of what to say, I pay a quick glance to Finn. He folds his arms across his chest, and his hands are clenched.

"Says the guy whose *family* visits him on the regular," Georgia fires back.

Gavin's eyes are cold when he shoots me a quick stare before he turns, walks into his office, and slams the door shut.

Rachelle stares at us, speechless.

Gavin needs to stop behaving like a child if he doesn't want the entire school to know he knocked me up.

Georgia winks at me.

The day after everone finding out about my pregnancy, I broke down and told her about Gavin. There was no way she'd allow me to keep it from her. We've been best friends for over a decade, and we have always confided in each other. Now, anytime she's around Gavin, she gives him shit.

"Let's go," I tell Finn.

Finn shoots Georgia and Rachelle a wave and follows me into the hallway. We pass banner- and poster-covered walls while heading toward my classroom. When we pass a line of fourth graders, they snicker and point to Finn.

"What's the principal's issue?" Finn asks when we walk inside the classroom. "Does he like you, or is he just a dick in general?"

"Just a dick in general," I reply.

He rubs at his lip as if questioning whether he should call me out on my bullshit. Finn is a pro at reading me. Eventually, I'll have to tell Finn the truth, but today, I want to have lunch with him and forget about Gavin.

"This is cute," he says, taking in my classroom. "It screams Grace."

Finn helped me move all my supplies in, but he hasn't seen it since I started for the year. A large bulletin board is decorated with positivity quotes and art displays, and I have posters covering the walls.

I've wanted to be a teacher since grade school. Some kids might have grown out of that phase but not me. My parents weren't excited at first, being their occupations pay more than a teacher's salary. There also isn't room for advancement unless I obtain a higher degree and become a professor.

My father is a judge, and my mother's a professor. Faith is an attorney. Even though this wasn't the career they hoped for me, they're supportive of my job. They've never once made me feel like my job isn't as important as theirs.

Finn grips the edge of a desk and starts to drag it toward mine, but I stop him. I smile and take the one next to him. He scoots his closer to mine.

"I like your new look," I tell him.

I wanted to punch Gavin just for ruining my moment of eye-screwing Finn when I walked into the office. I love Finn in every look, but him dressed up, looking like he's ready to take care of business, is hot. Although I prefer his casual look—because it's him—it's nice to see him mix it up. He's like me now, having different business and fun clothes.

He grins, pulling at the collar of his blue button-up. "I'm trying to fit the part of a man who sells hundred-thousand-dollar cars."

"You fit the part, and you are, no doubt, the hottest car dealer there."

He wipes his thumb over his jaw. "When I sell my first car, I'm taking you out for a kick-ass dinner." He jerks his thumb toward my belly. "And buying whatever you need for the little one."

My heart warms at his comment.

Butterflies swarm in my stomach.

He's not lying.

Finn would do anything for me ... or my baby.

My cheeks are heated when I point at the bag. "What's on the menu?"

He grins, holding up the bag. "Bistro Bella."

"Mmm. My favorite."

My stomach growls when he pulls out two sandwiches and settles one on my desk. Next comes a bag of Cheetos and a Sprite.

All my favorites.

"How's your day going?" he asks as I unwrap my egglant and ranch sub. He hasn't touched his food yet. All his attention is on me.

I shrug, ripping open the Cheetos. "Same ole, same ole."

"How are you feeling?"

"Let's just say, pregnancy is not a fun party."

He chuckles, opening his veggie sub. He's kept meat away from me since the day I told him it made me nauseas.

"How's the first day at the new j-o-b."

"It's, uh ... different."

Different.

Not good.

Not bad.

Indifferent.

I smear my finger through a ranch glob on the wrapper. "If you don't like it, don't stay there. I didn't expect you to take that job."

"What do you expect from me?"

His question startles me.

"I didn't mean to sound like an asshole." He reaches out and caresses my arm. "It's me genuinely asking what you need from me to make you happy during this. Whatever it is, it's yours."

I take a giant bite of my sandwich, hoping to swallow it along with my emotions. I sniffle and frown. These damn pregnancy hormones are getting the best of me. I cry at nearly everything these days.

Cheerios commercials.

When I chose the wrong color for my manicure.

When Snooki got arrested during a *Jersey Shore* rerun.

I take a sip of my Sprite. "I want you to do whatever you're comfortable with."

"I'm comfortable with whatever. You call the shots." He pops a Cheetos in his mouth.

"I shouldn't call the shots when you're the one doing me a favor."

"Like you haven't done me favors throughout the years? You're one of my closest friends, Grace. If you need something as simple as that—"

"Simple?" I shake my head. "What I'm asking from you isn't simple. I'm asking you to lie and pretty much put your life on hold."

He drops his sandwich to give me his full attention. "Babe, if lying is what you need from me, I'll lie all the way to hell. Tell me what a normal baby daddy does, and I'm there."

———

"SWEAR TO GOD, if Gavin keeps this shit up, I'm hiding mice in his office ... or at least giving him a swift kick in the balls," Georgia says. "You could easily get him fired for what he did."

It's the end of the school day, and we stopped by our favorite smoothie place before going home. With everything going on and her no longer being my roommate, it's harder for us to catch up.

Georgia and I met in middle school when she transferred, and I was her tour guide. She was the quirkiness to my shyness.

Since Cohen practically raised her, she spent a lot of time at my house while he was working to support them. Lola joined our group during our junior year. Like Georgia, she was a transfer. I'd turned a guy down at a party who was giving me a hard time, and Lola jumped in to set him straight. Since then, the three of us have referred to ourselves as The Three Musketeers. My life would be boring and lonelier if it wasn't for them.

I shake my head. "They'd most likely fire us both. Damage control would be easier if everyone involved was gone."

I shudder at the thought of losing my job. I love it at Sunset Hill. I was there first, so if anyone needs to go, it should be Gavin. I'm not sure if the school board would look at it that way, though.

"That's messed up." Georgia pulls her brown curls that are blowing in the wind into a ponytail. "You should tell his wife."

"Trust me, I've thought about it." *Too many times.* "But what good would it do?"

"Get his ass in trouble, is the good it'd do. Make his wife leave him and take half his shit." She points at me with her cup. "If he pulls that shit again, threaten to tell his wife ... or better yet, *I will.* Don't let him ruin the good thing you have with Finn."

I blow out a breath. "What do you mean, good thing?"

"Finn is an amazing man," she says with such certainty it's as if she's stating her blood type.

"He is ... but ..." I trail off, unsure of how to explain my feelings about the situation.

She raises a brow. "But what?"

"It's not like we have a real relationship ... or that he's actually the father of the baby. In the end, he'll leave, and I'll be a single mother."

It's scary, doing it alone, but I've come to terms that it'll be my new life. At least on the bright side, there will be no baby-name fights. I try to rid those thoughts, knowing I'll still have my family and friends.

"Why can't it be real?" she asks. "Finn might not be the biological father, but you two have liked each other for years. Look how he's stepping up. I'm sure he'd be okay with being the dad—"

"He's *playing* the dad. It's a role." I keep reminding myself this so the hurt won't be so deep when he leaves.

Her face softens. "It's not a role to him. He's doing things where you don't have audiences to act in front of. Give him a chance."

"Not only am I pregnant"—I glance down as shame hits my cheek—"but I'm also weird." A sour taste forms in my mouth, and I push my smoothie away as nausea creeps in. This subject always makes me want to puke ... and hide.

Georgia holds up a finger. "First of all, you're not weird. Weird is choosing Nick Carter over Justin Timberlake or thinking *Sister Wives* isn't creepy." She signals toward me. "You, my best friend, are not weird."

"You were my roommate." I bite into my lower lip. "You know how I am."

It's a reason I wanted to kill Faith when she mentioned Finn moving in with me. Other than the nightmare the other night, I haven't had many incidents lately.

She reaches across the table and presses her hand over mine. "You went through something that was fucked up, and you have PTSD. It's common, and Finn would understand. He cares about you. I mean, would any random man sign up to put his life on hold like this?"

I release a heavy sigh. "I know; I know."

A smile plays at her lips. "Now, make him yours and stop being afraid."

# CHAPTER SEVENTEEN

---

# Finn

AS BAD AS I want to turn my phone off, I can't.

I'm always nervous something will happen.

My dad's name flashes across my phone for what seems like the hundredth time. Since he's already left three voicemails, I know what he wants, but I'm at work. He'll have to wait until I get off. I won't risk this job to deal with his messes.

He's shown up to Twisted Fox countless times when I haven't answered his calls. He's made scenes, asked for free liquor, and once started a fight with a man over a game of pool. The less he knows about my life, the better. Otherwise, he never fails to make his existence known when he wants something. No way am I risking that embarrassment here.

Hell, he'd probably come in drunk, asking to test-drive a BMW.

I wait until my lunch break to return his call.

"Quit blowing up my phone while I'm working," I hiss as soon as he answers.

"At work?" he huffs. "It's too damn early for you to be at work. I called, and they said you weren't there. Not to mention, you never go into work during the day." He lowers his voice, forcing it to sound sad. "Why are you lying to your own flesh and blood?"

"I got a new job—a day job."

"Ah, where?"

"None of your business."

"That's rude." He releases another huff, and knowing him, he's scowling. "As your father, I should know. What if there's an emergency?"

I sink deeper into the seat of my car and tip my head back, resting it against the headrest. "Do what you always do. Leave messages, and I'll get back with you. Most of the time, your *emergencies* don't constitute as *emergencies*."

"Me going hungry isn't an emergency?"

His response sends a fire through my blood. "You're not going hungry. I bought groceries for you earlier this week."

"I need something new. I can't make food all the time." He pauses as if searching for the right words for his next request. "Order me a pizza."

"Gotta go." I hang up.

---

"YO! FINN!" Lincoln greets me with a smile from the other side of the bar when I sink down on a barstool.

Lincoln collects bills off the bar on his way toward me. He hasn't worked at Twisted Fox long and recently joined our circle of friends. He's Archer's brother, and he was recently released from federal prison.

Their father had started doing shady shit with the family business. While Archer left to avoid trouble, Lincoln stayed, attempting to turn his dad straight. When the feds showed up, Lincoln had refused to feed them information about his father, which led him to being charged with crimes.

When he was released, Archer hired him to bartend

here. Then, Cassidy was going through her own trouble, and now, they're dating. Lincoln recently asked Cassidy to move in with him, but after Grace revealed she was pregnant, Cassidy told Lincoln she couldn't leave her without a roommate.

The memory of Faith asking me about moving in with Grace smacks into me. Grace hasn't brought it up since our dinner, so I'm not sure how she feels about it. Since Cassidy refused to leave Grace without a roommate, Lincoln practically lives there now too.

"What can I get you?" Lincoln asks.

I drum my fingers along the bar. "A Coors is good."

It's the first time I've actually had someone serve me here. Normally, I walk behind the bar, snag what I want, and pay for it.

Turning, he grabs a bottle from the fridge, pops off the cap, and slides it to me. "How's the new job? Miss us yet?"

I chuckle. "The new job is going well. It's different, but I'm getting used to it."

"Luxury Imports is a good-ass dealership. I bought cars from there before my life fell apart."

I'm convinced Lincoln isn't normal as he laughs. Even though he went to prison for a crime he technically hadn't committed, only witnessed and hadn't snitched, he doesn't have a chip on his shoulder that I'd definitely have. Sometimes, I'm jealous of how well he handles the shit that's gone bad in the past.

He leans back on his heels and shoves his hands into his pockets. "If I ever decide to trade it in on something new, I'll holler at you."

I smile. "Thanks, man."

I sold my third car today, and when I added the commission I'd receive, I nearly fell out of my chair. It's more than I'd make in a month working anywhere else. The amount some people spend on cars baffles me. Hell, I could buy a house with that kind of money.

Some of my coworkers have lightened up their asshole attitudes—most likely after somehow finding out that I'm the father of his sister-in-law's baby.

*Did Brian tell them that?*

I'm sure they talk a lot of shit behind my back, though. Assholes just don't want to get fired. Not that I'd ask Brian to can a guy for not liking me.

Lincoln slaps his palm along the bar. "You're actually just the person I wanted to talk to."

I take a swig of my beer. "What's up?"

He shoves his hand through his short black hair. "Cass might kill me for telling you this, but ..." He pauses, looking from each side of the bar, double-checking she's not here to kick his ass. "She's pregnant."

I wait to read his reaction before replying.

*Is this good or bad news to him?*

From the shit-eating grin on his face and the way he's practically bouncing on his toes, I'm going with good news.

I smile. "Congrats, man."

He chuckles. "There must be something in that townhouse's water or some roommate ovaries wanting to get knocked up at the same time."

He taps his fingers along the bar. "And that's why I want to talk to you."

I hold my hands out in a jokingly innocent gesture. "It wasn't me, I swear."

Leaning across the bar, he pushes my shoulder. "Real funny, jackass."

He stares at me, unblinking. "A two-bedroom townhouse isn't going to work unless the babies want their nursery in the living room."

"Okay," I slowly drawl the word out.

"Grace told Cass that her sister mentioned you moving in with her."

"Okay," I repeat in the same tone as before.

He frowns that I'm not feeding his conversation yet before perking up his shoulders. "Well, buddy, now comes the time when you help everyone out and become Grace's new roommate."

I stiffen in my chair.

"We have an empty penthouse after Archer and Georgia moved out. Before, I didn't mind staying at the townhouse. Grace is cool, but now, I'd like some room to start a family. We won't move out until Grace has another roommate, and she mentioned to Cassidy there was talk of you doing that. Is it something you're really considering?"

I cover my face with my hand. "Looks like I'd better talk to Grace."

---

IT TURNS OUT, Lincoln asking me to take their roommate position was perfect timing.

After I left Twisted Fox, my dad's landlord, Roger, called, notifying me that my dad wouldn't leave. Unbeknownst to me, he'd evicted my father months ago, and he was done with allowing him to squat at his rental, free of charge.

Muttering every curse in the book, I got into my car.

Thirty minutes later, I'm pulling into the driveway of the rental my father apparently isn't paying for. He's on the lawn, arguing with Roger ... and next to them stand two police officers.

*Great.*

This isn't the first time I've dealt with the police regarding my father. I'm sure it won't be the last either.

All eyes are on me as I step out of my car.

"You called him, you son of a bitch?" my dad snarls to Roger before flipping him the bird with both hands.

Roger, a thin man with balding hair, pushes up his thin-framed glasses. "What was I supposed to do, John? You won't leave!"

My father stomps his foot like a third grader who lost the kickball game. "This is between us." He swings his arm out. "Yet you called the police and my son."

"The neighbors called the police because you were throwing stuff out the front door and threatening to beat me up," Roger deadpans.

My temples throb as I join the group. "Dad, leave him alone. It was his last resort. This is your fault for not paying your rent."

He should be grateful Roger has put up with him this long.

"Thank you." Roger exhales a long breath.

I nod, a hint of sympathy in my eyes. My dad is a lot to handle and never makes life easy on anyone. He's a landlord's nightmare, and he can't keep a place to save his life. When I was growing up, we moved at least three times a year, jumping place to place, dodging landlords.

I turn to Roger, ignoring my father's outburst behind me. "Where do we go from here?" My mouth turns dry in regret as I pull out my wallet. "How much does he owe?"

My father's shit-talking stops. He sees a way out now, another scheme not to have to pay his rent and have me cover for him—*again*.

"He's three months behind," Roger replies with a shake of his head.

"Two months, motherfucker!" my dad yells to my back.

"Three months," Roger states. "He kept promising to have the money to pay the back rent, but then I realized that wasn't happening. That's when I delivered an eviction notice a month ago, and he still won't leave."

"Three months ... so six grand?" I ask.

Roger nods. "If you don't count late fees."

"Can I pay it?" I'll have to dip into my savings, but I don't know what else to do.

Roger shuffles his feet against the grass. "Don't worry about that. It's his responsibility, not yours. Even if he paid every cent he owes, he can't move back in. I won't deal with him anymore, and I rented it to another tenant. I already have to deal with him trashing the place—cigarette burns and stains on the carpet, holes in the walls, and the bedroom door is somehow missing."

"It's not that bad!" my dad yells, stepping closer to Roger and thrusting his finger in his face. "And I'd better get my goddamn deposit back."

I grab the collar of my dad's shirt and jerk him back before the cops do. "Go pack your shit, and let's go."

"Screw that!" Spit flies from my dad's mouth as he speaks. "My TV is in there! My bed! I ain't letting him sell that."

"No one is taking your shit," I say, raising my voice. "We'll get it moved either to my place or a storage unit."

My dad smirks at Roger. "Damn straight, we will. Don't be putting your hands on my things."

I pinch the bridge of my nose. "Dad, get your ass in your car and drive to my place unless you want to be sleeping on the street tonight." I turn to Roger. "I'll arrange for his shit to be picked up."

With a slew of curses, he does as I said, slamming his door and glaring at us.

"I'm sorry, Roger. I'll mail you a check for the back rent," I tell the middle-aged man before turning to the officers. "Thanks for coming out."

Jesse, the chief of police who's dealt with my father one too many times, tugs at his ear. "As rude as this sounds, I hope this is the last time I see your father."

"Same," I say.

"Maybe him finding a place out of town will help him stay out of trouble," he continues. "Get him away from the bad crowd he hangs out with. If he goes to jail again, he might be in there a while."

"I'll see what I can do."

Jesse slaps me on the back. "Be safe, and good luck, Finn."

---

I STEP OUTSIDE to my patio and call Grace. As much as I want to talk face-to-face, I'm keeping an eye on my dad until he calms his ass down.

There's a sense of relief that I didn't have to give Roger six thousand dollars but then came the predicament of finding my dad somewhere to stay. His credit is terrible, so it'll be a struggle to find someone to rent to him, especially if they reach out to past landlords for references.

My only options are to throw him out on the street, drop him off at a homeless shelter, or make my apartment his homeless shelter. Since I'd feel like an ass going with either of the first two, I choose the last. The problem is, we'd last maybe ten minutes living together before a fight erupted. I can let him stay there, and since Lincoln told me he and Cassidy were game for crashing at the penthouse, I can see if I can stay there until I find a new place for my father.

Let's pray that my dad doesn't fuck my place up like he did the others.

The first person I call is Lincoln, telling him that I need somewhere to crash and asking if he and Cassidy were cool to sleep at the penthouse for a few days. Cassidy is with him, and they say they're fine with it.

My next call goes to Grace.

"Hello?" she answers.

"Hey." I plop down on a patio chair, crossing my ankles in front of me. "How are you feeling?" It's the first question I always ask now.

"Pregnant," she replies with a laugh. "But not too bad. I just devoured ten Oreos, so that always helps."

"Oreos always save the day." I chuckle and scratch my cheek.

Asking for favors isn't something I'm good at, nor is it something I do on the regular. At times, I have an ego issue. Not the type of egotistical guy who has a big head on his shoulders and thinks he's the shit. I hide behind a false ego so people don't see my struggle.

"And you?" she asks, breaking me away from my thoughts.

"It was okay." I choose against telling her about my dad nightmare and scuff my shoes against the concrete. "Can I ask you a favor? And you can say no if you're not cool with it."

"Of course. You can always ask me for anything."

I puff out a breath. "Remember how Faith suggested I stay with you?"

"I remember my overbearing sister asking this, yes." She laughs.

"My dad needs somewhere to stay, and I offered him my apartment. Since I have a one-bedroom and Cass said I could take her bed, are you okay with me staying a few nights until we find him somewhere else?"

"My house is always open to you," Grace says with no hesitation.

---

WALKING IN THE LIVING ROOM, I find my dad slouched on the couch, chomping on barbecue potato chips with his dirty tennis shoes propped up on the glass coffee table.

"You need to restock the kitchen," he says, holding up the bag. "Too many healthy options for a man like me."

"You can go to the grocery store if you don't like what I have." I stand in front of him and cross my arms. "You ready to explain why you haven't been paying your rent?"

He wipes his chip-greasy hands onto his jeans. "That's none of your business."

"When you're evicted and crashing at my place, it sure is."

Not that I'll get the truth.

I'm sure he'll feed me some bullshit excuse.

"It's not easy, paying bills," he replies, cracking his knuckles. "I struggle."

This is the part where I used to feel bad for him.

Now, I know he's a liar.

"How are you struggling if you don't pay the bills that are supposedly the reason you're struggling?"

He only shrugs, pops a chip in his mouth, and loudly munches on it.

"You get plenty of money from your Social Security— enough to pay your bills."

I stare at my father—a man I've embarrassingly never looked up to. As the years have passed, his appearance has deteriorated. In my teens, he was a drunk, but all the liquor and drug use has taken a toll on him. He's lanky, his cheeks are sunken, and his clothes are baggy. His hair—with a large receding hairline—is oily.

I collapse onto the couch. "Dad, do you want to get some help?"

As usual, he snarls at my question. "I don't need nothing from anyone."

I hold out my hand. "Dad—"

"No!" he screams, shoving the bag of chips onto the couch. "I ain't having this conversation with you."

I wouldn't consider my father a junkie, but I could be

wrong. He isn't high every time I see him, but it's getting worse each time. But there's no denying that he does his fair share of using.

With a groan, he pulls himself to his feet. "I need to shower."

---

"DON'T MESS ANYTHING UP," I tell my father.

Even though I've lived in the same apartment for years, I do a quick scan of the living room, taking in every inch of it. I rented a one-bedroom so people wouldn't attempt to move in with me.

No one wants to rest their head on a couch every night.

Call it an asshole move, but us living together would result in nothing but endless fights. He'd have wanted to take the easy road—live with me, not pay a penny, and blow his money on bullshit. My plan was for him to finance himself, although that didn't seem to work out. Now, he's here, in my one-bedroom apartment, while I'm finding somewhere else to crash.

It's small, but I've made the place nice, made it mine ... with Grace's help. Hell, she made most of the selections. We'd go shopping, and she'd pick shit out.

The floors are a dark hardwood and the walls beige. A deep-set taupe leather sectional is in the middle of the living room with matching coffee and end tables. A black shag rug sits in the middle of the living room. A few framed photos are on the tables—all with Grace and me, or my friends and me. There's a small kitchen with a four-seater table. I don't spend much time here because I like to stay out, stay busy.

"Oh, don't you worry." My dad smirks. "I'll take good care of the place."

There was no controlling his smile when I told him he could crash at the apartment *for two weeks* and I'd stay somewhere else. He never asked where I'd stay or if it'd cost me anything. All he cared about was his ass being covered.

I'll still need to check on him regularly to ensure he doesn't have visitors or fuck my shit up.

Earlier, I packed up all the crap I didn't want him touching and stuffed it into the trunk of my car. Grabbing my bag, I throw it over my shoulder, give him one last warning, and tell him to call me if he needs anything before leaving and making my way to Grace's.

# CHAPTER EIGHTEEN

## Grace

FINN MOVING IN IS a blessing in disguise.

I had no reservations about telling Finn yes when he asked to stay at the townhouse. With Lincoln and Cassidy working at night more, I'll feel protected with him here. The downside is my fear of him discovering my secret. So far, throughout the years, I've done well with hiding it, but the more people around means the higher my risk is of being exposed.

Georgia and Lola know. Cassidy and Lincoln have their suspicions, but I've always brushed off any concern. With Finn knowing me so well, with him caring about me so deeply, I'm uncertain if he'll allow any *brushing off*.

Finn has a way of cracking open the shell I've kept glued together for so long.

He's a man who can read me as if we shared the same brain. He knows when something is wrong, even when I try to hide it. He knows when something is deeper than what I'm letting on. There's no doubt in my mind that Finn is my soul mate.

The soul mate I can't have.

I've also never lived with a man before.

Finn texted me five minutes ago to let me know he's headed my way.

Snatching my phone from my bathroom vanity, I call Faith.

"What if Finn staying here is a mistake?" I ask. "I didn't consider what would happen if I had an episode."

"Grace," Faith says my name with sympathy and understanding. "You've done well with them the past few years, and last time, you didn't freak out. You called me. Having Finn there will most likely help with them. Like Brian does with me."

"If he finds out, it'll be mortifying," I croak, sitting on the closed toilet seat.

"Let's say he does. I bet you a new Gucci bag he won't judge you for it."

"He won't judge me to my face, but he could think I'm strange." I wrinkle my nose. "And nope with betting you another bag. You always win."

She laughs. "And you know I'll for sure win this one."

"Yeah, yeah, yeah," I mutter.

"Everything will be fine."

I slide off the toilet at the knock on my front door. "He's here. Pray for me."

"Quit overthinking and have fun with your fake baby daddy. If you need anything, I'm only one call away.

"Oh my God, you're crazy, and I'm sure you're happy that you're getting your way with this."

"Absolutely I am. Thank you, Finn's dad. Give me the address, and I'll send a fruit basket."

---

BEING ALONE with Finn isn't out of the ordinary.

Him temporarily living with me? That's a different story.

It's not that I don't feel comfortable around him. I'm just uncertain of where this will take us. We've been dipping our toes into such new territory lately—fake dating, him playing my baby daddy, now us staying together. This has been a month of twists and turns.

A sense of disappointment hits me when he walks through the front door with only a duffel bag thrown over his shoulder. He packed light as though this is only temporary and he's scared of asking for too much. I wasn't expecting a moving truck, but a duffel bag seems too fleeting. Deep in my heart, I already know it'll hurt when he returns to his place.

He swings the bag off his shoulder and grips the strap. "I'm going to toss this in Cassidy's room."

I nod with a smile and head into the kitchen for a glass of water.

Finn meets me. "I really appreciate you letting me stay here."

"Always," I reply.

"Does this mean I get the roommate hot chocolate you girls always talk about?"

Georgia and I started the *roomie hot chocolate* when we first moved in together. We created the perfect spiked hot chocolate recipe and drank them from mugs with our faces on them. When she moved out and Cassidy moved in, I got a mug for her, and that was our drink we made once a week. As a joke, we bought Lincoln one when he started staying with us on the regular.

"I can make you one," I tell him. "And a virgin for yours truly."

"Shit, I need to quit forgetting you can't drink."

"Geesh, you say that like I'm an alcoholic or something."

He jerks his head back, and his shoulders stiffen at my comment. "Nah, I know alcoholics, and that's not you." Gone is the playfulness he had.

Finn doesn't show his emotional side often. He's a pro at

maintaining the *cool and fun guy* image, but like me, sometimes, the things we want to hide the most shine through the cracks.

Even though it's never been brought up, I'm certain there is alcoholism or addiction in his family. He never drinks more than two beers, I've never seen him drunk, and he's the closest with the one friend in our group who doesn't drink.

As bad as I've wanted to poke at Finn's head until I picked everything out, I need to wait until he's ready to tell me—that he fully wants to open himself up and release what pains him.

"What if we skip the drink and have a roomie pizza instead?" I suggest, tilting my head to the side and meeting his gaze.

His shoulders slump as if a weight has been lifted. "Pizza sounds damn good."

Since neither of us wants to fix a pizza, we order one. I change out of my maxi dress into sweats and join Finn in the living room, taking the opposite side of the couch from him.

"I meant what I said, Grace. I'm here for you if you need anything. You name it, and I'm there. You never have to do anything alone."

For a moment, he's rendered me speechless. Finn has always been helpful, always told me he's here for me, no matter what, but this goes deeper than before. He's laying it out there —that he's not only there for me but also my baby. There's nothing Finn would refuse me.

That's not me bragging.

It's me knowing that I've never been in love with a man, and I will never love a man as I do him. Even if I searched high and low, Finn has a heart that no one else has—one filled with forgiveness, which is more than I deserve.

We eat pizza. We watch Netflix.

When I go to bed, my nerves spiral.

*Please let this be a normal night for me.*

# CHAPTER NINETEEN

## Finn

THERE'S A SCREAM.

A loud, piercing scream.

I jump out of bed and sprint out of the bedroom.

Rushing down the hall, I follow the second scream to Grace's bedroom. Wiggling the doorknob, I find it locked.

"Grace!" I shout, pounding on the door in a panic. "Grace! Open up!"

The screaming stops.

My hands are shaking as I draw in deep breaths. The door-knob moves, and Grace flings the door open. A dim light in her bedroom allows me to see the expression on her beautiful face.

It's fear.

Torment.

Expressions I've never witnessed coming from her.

A tear runs down her cheek.

"Are you okay?" My voice is harder than it should be, but I'm fucking scared.

She's staring straight ahead, but it's like she can't see me.

Staring into nothing.

I snap my fingers in front of her.

She blinks as if powering back on and stares at me blankly.

I slip by her, barging into the bedroom to see if there's anyone I need to kill.

"A nightmare," she chokes out. "I had a nightmare."

Whipping around, I watch the recognition dawn on her face of what happened. She takes slow steps to her bed and sits on the edge. I do another sweep of her room and verify the closet and bathroom are empty. I don't want to seem overbearing, but I've never heard someone yell like that over a nightmare.

After confirming I'm not about to kick someone's ass, I sit down next to her, leaving a few inches between us. Her hand is pressed to her chest, and her eyes are brimmed with tears. Her breathing is ragged, and she works hard to control it.

I wait until she calms.

Wait until she looks at me.

But she only does the first.

Reaching out, I tenderly take her hand. "Are the nightmares a normal thing ... or is it because I'm here?" My body turns rigid with tension as I await her response.

I shut my eyes, and it hits me. All the times that Georgia and Cassidy said they couldn't leave Grace alone. Her hating the dark and staying at her parents' whenever they worked late.

I always took it as a woman not wanting to stay home alone —which is understandable. Especially since Georgia's form of a good time is murder documentaries.

"I wouldn't say normal ..." She shrugs, forcing herself to appear nonchalant. "I get them when I'm stressed."

My pounding heart relaxes when she half-turns to face me.

At least it's something.

Better than her staring at the damn wall.

"It's not you being here, I promise," she says, her face pale. "They just happen sometimes."

I nod, another question popping up inside my head. "Do you always sleep with your door locked?"

"It's something I've done since my teens and not because I'm uncomfortable with you here."

"Are you okay? You want me to grab you water? Anything?"

She shakes her head. "I'm okay."

"I'm right down the hall." I point toward the door.

Her face grows paler.

I change course, slightly stuttering as I struggle to find the right words. "If you're not up for going back to bed, we can watch a movie?"

"You work early in the morning."

"Babe, I'm used to staying up late and surviving on limited sleep. If you need me awake, I'm awake."

She quietly exhales. "A movie sounds good."

She climbs back under her comforter, and I take the space beside her, not getting underneath the covers. Instead of a movie, she turns on a show we've seen countless times. As she slowly falls asleep, I'm hit with a wave of uncertainty.

*Do I return to my bedroom?*

I can't lock the door behind me.

Instead of leaving her, I stay next to her—on top of the blankets—and fall asleep, hoping she doesn't freak out in the morning.

---

"I'M KIND OF EMBARRASSED," Grace tells me the next morning.

The sun shining through her curtains woke me early, before her, and I tiptoed to my bedroom before she woke up. I showered, got dressed, and was in the kitchen, waiting for her.

Her face appears refreshed as if she got a full eight hours when she appears. Her hair is thrown back into a braid, and her baby bump is starting to show through her dress. I've never dated or been with a pregnant woman, but I find a baby bump on Grace to be sexy as hell.

"Nah." I take a sip of my coffee. "We all have nightmares. I had them bad as a kid because my father found it normal to watch horror movies with me while I was growing up. I get it."

The only difference is, Grace wasn't scared of the bogeyman, or Jason, or Freddy Krueger. The terror on her face alerted me that it was deeper than your typical nightmare.

A blush stings her cheeks. "Thank you for being there for me."

"I told you, if you need me, I'm there."

*No matter what.*

# CHAPTER TWENTY

# Grace

I'M a pregnant woman walking into the city's hottest nightclub.

Something I never anticipated happening.

I expect judgmental stares, but thankfully, no one seems to notice.

Since my baby bump is starting to show, I went with a loose-fitting maxi dress and sandals tonight. Not that the dress is out of the ordinary. Comfortable is my style. My friends have labeled my style as *sophisticated flower child*.

Colorful strobe lights and loud music blare through the crowded club. Finn and I maneuver through the bodies hand in hand. We pass a group of people yelling at each other over the music and stop at the VIP section. The bouncer jerks his head toward Finn and allows us entry.

We don't go clubbing often, but since it's Lola's birthday, we all made an exception. Normally, we tend to hang out at someone's house or go to dinner, only really going for a night out if it's someone's birthday or we have something big to celebrate. I'm grateful Lola got us a table so we can hang out. I hate bumping into bodies while holding a conversation, and I have the rhythm of a three-year-old jamming to "Old Town Road," so the dance floor is out of the question.

Riding with Finn is common for me on nights like this. I prefer leaving early, and he never minds taking me home when I'm ready. Not that my friends wouldn't, but I hate being the buzzkill of the party.

Our friends are seated around the booth except for Lola and Georgia, who are semi-dancing in the corner. Purses, glasses, bottles of liquor, and a bucket of ice are scattered along the table.

"There's the baby daddy and baby mama," Lincoln says when we come into view.

"Grace!" Lola shouts, stumbling toward us. "My bestie carrying my future godchild. Thank you for being here!"

"Um, excuse you," Georgia says from behind her. "I'm the future godmother."

Lola wrinkles her nose. "We can *all* be a godparent." Her speech is slightly slurred.

The birthday girl doesn't get drunk often. Silas is sober, so she tends not to drink much. Not that Silas would care if she did. He's always up for clubbing. No one knows *why* he doesn't drink, but I don't think it's addiction.

Georgia shrugs. "I'll accept that."

Georgia, sporting a sequined crop top and jeans, squeezes into the spot next to Archer. Her boyfriend appears as happy to be clubbing as I do visiting my OB/GYN.

"Happy Birthday," I greet Lola, dropping Finn's hand to hug her.

Everyone is relaxed in their space. Jamie and Cohen are next to each other, and Jamie is showing him something on her phone. Their attendance is surprising. With the two kids—one being a baby—and Jamie's crazy hours in the ER, they don't get out much. Georgia and Archer are snuggled together, her leg over thigh. Lincoln has his arm thrown over Cassidy's shoulders while she sips on water. Maliki and Sierra, our friends who live in Blue Beech, are laughing with drinks in their hands. Maliki once hung out with us more, but he returned to his hometown to take over his father's bar. Sierra is Cassidy's older sister and the one who helped her get a job at Twisted Fox. Silas, the only one not on the couch, is sprawled out on a chair next to everyone as if he's the king of the party.

Finn helps me onto the couch before sinking into the space next to me on the end.

I gape at Lola. "I haven't seen you this wasted since college."

"I've *never* seen her this wasted, period," Silas says. He spoke to me, but his eyes warily stay on Lola. He hasn't been as loud or as playful as he usually is tonight.

"Agreed." Georgia nods next to me. "Did something happen today?"

Lola shakes her head, her eyes heavy-lidded. "It's my birthday. I was gifted a complimentary bottle from the club since I'm the owner's alcohol rep. He also sent over some bubblegum shooters." She motions to the tray of shooters, snags one, and knocks it back.

The birthday girl definitely looks gorgeous in her short black dress and red stiletto pumps. Her dark hair is straight and parted down the middle, a rhinestone pin clipped to the side. I've always considered my style boring compared to her edginess. Her style changes from day to day, and she can get away with it.

Silas runs his hand through his dark hair in frustration. "I'll be sure to inform Phil you're cut off."

Lola rolls her eyes. "Buzzkill."

"This is weird," I tell Finn underneath my breath.

"Them at odds?" he asks.

"They never argue."

Our waitress interrupts us to take more drink orders.

"Just a water?" I ask Finn when he tells the waiter he'll have a seltzer water like me.

He grins down at me. "I figured you should have a sober buddy."

I sneakily point to Cassidy. "She's not drinking either, and the past few times I've seen her, she's been ordering the same drinks as me. I wonder if she's prego."

He shrugs. "It might be good to have a pregnancy buddy."

I give myself a mental reminder to ask. It can't happen here, and I need to figure out the best way to go about it. You always hear of those women who ask someone when they're due, only to find out they're not actually pregnant. I'd be mortified.

"My best friend." Lola's voice drags me away from our conversation. She topples into Silas's lap, sitting sideways, and wraps her arms around his neck.

This type of flirting is normal for them. Unlike Finn and me, they've never held back their desire for the other. Although they swear they've never acted on it. They find it normal, *as friends*, to sit on each other's laps, dance together, and share a bed.

At times, I wish I could be as brave as her. To flirt with Finn and not be scared of judgment or rejection.

Lola tips her head down, her dark hair becoming a curtain around their faces. I covet the confidence she has. The girl gives no fucks.

My hand clamps over my mouth when she shifts and straddles him.

"Holy shit," Georgia mutters at the same time Finn says, "That's a new one."

Cohen leans in. "I've never seen it go that far between them."

All eyes are on them. Lola whispers in Silas's ear. Sierra, the closest to them, scoots in closer to eavesdrop.

"Are they about to bang right there?" Lincoln asks when Lola grinds into Silas's lap.

"Nah," Archer states matter-of-factly. "Those two play mind games with each other." He dances his fingers over Georgia's thigh. "Remember when we used to do that shit, babe?"

Georgia tilts her head to the side. "Mind games wasn't straddling and grinding against you."

"This won't end well," Finn says. "She's drunk, and Silas is annoyed."

I steer my attention back to tonight's entertainment. Silas's shoulders are rigid, and his jaw is clenched. He's anchored his hands to Lola's hips, halting her from grinding more as they converse. The serious expression on his face tells me to look away, but I can't. I gasp when Lola grips Silas's hand and drags it down to her thigh.

Silas abruptly stands, his face hot with a fury I've never witnessed from him, causing Lola to drop onto the floor.

"Goddammit, Lola," he huffs, a wince spreading across his whole face, and he raises his voice. "Drink some water because you're being a sloppy fucking drunk." As soon as the words leave his mouth, regret flashes across his face.

Everyone is silent, watching this play out.

"Come on." He puts his hand out to help her up, but she pushes it away.

Lola's eyes water as she pulls herself to her feet. "No, I don't want your help."

"I'm sorry." His voice breaks.

"I think you should go." She adjusts her dress and folds her arms over her stomach while failing to meet anyone's gaze. "That's what I want from you for my birthday. To leave." This is the most vulnerable I've ever seen Lola.

"Fine." Silas pinches the bridge of his nose. "I'll go."

Just as he turns to walk away, we hear," Well, well, look what we have here," come from a voice I don't recognize.

I shift in my seat and find a man I've never seen before standing at the head of the table, running his hands together. Two guys stand behind him, a few inches back, like they're his right-hand men. He's tall with dark hair and a clean-shaven face. Even though he's not wearing an expensive suit and tie, his casual clothes are just as pricey as what they would cost.

"Uh-oh," Finn says. "This night might get worse than it already was."

"What do you mean?" I ask without glancing at him.

The guy rubs his hands together. "Silas fucking Malone."

Silas slowly turns to face the mystery man and icily stares him down. He steps to the side to block off Lola from the guy's view.

The man moves in closer and strokes his jaw. "I haven't seen you in forever. You act as if your family doesn't exist."

"I'm a busy man," Silas says, his tone challenging.

"Busy, huh?" he scoffs, scanning our area and taking in the surroundings. "Enough time for a birthday party though, huh? Who's the birthday someone?"

Lola steps around Silas. "Me."

The man runs his tongue over his lips. "Goddamn, the birthday girl is hot." He delivers a cocky smile while holding out his hand to her. "I'm Trent, Silas's brother."

"Stepbrother," Silas corrects with a snarl. "No blood relation. Thank fucking God."

"Oh, come on, brother," Trent mocks. "Let's forget about the past. How about this? Let's share a drink. We can go to my table —which is larger and surrounded by NBA and NFL players and other high-profile people—or stay here."

Silas works his jaw. "Nah, we're good. Go hang out with your high-profile friends and beat feet."

Trent doesn't pay Silas a glance. Lola has all of his attention. "At least let me buy the birthday girl a drink."

"She's had enough to drink," Silas snaps, popping his knuckles.

Archer hauls himself to his feet, joining Silas, and Lincoln does the same. Trent chuckles at Silas now having his right-hand men.

Lola chews on her lower lip. "I wouldn't mind a birthday Sprite, though. I don't want to be hungover tomorrow."

"I think you've already crossed that line," Silas says.

Trent snaps his fingers. "A birthday Sprite it is." He does a sweeping gesture toward the table. "Any of these guys your boyfriend?"

His eyes level on Silas, no doubt knowing his reaction to Trent's flirtation will be a sign that Silas likes her.

Lola doesn't cast one glance toward Silas before answering, "Nope."

Silas curses under his breath and wipes his forehead with the back of his arm.

This isn't Lola.

She's not spiteful.

She'd never want to purposely hurt Silas.

*What is going on with them?*

I can't blame her, though. She has to be hurting from Silas's rejection. She's prideful, someone not typically turned down. If I was coming down from the rejection of a lifetime, of a man practically dumping me on the floor, I'd take that Sprite offered by a dreamy man.

Our waitress comes scrambling toward us, nearly tripping on her heels, holding a tray of drinks. "Sorry! I got caught up at a table."

"Totally fine," I say, taking my seltzer water and handing Finn his.

She turns and halts when she notices Trent. "Hey, Trent. Can I get you something?" She giggles.

"Nah, I'm good, Abby." He wiggles his fingers toward Lola,

causing Abby to frown. "I'm going to escort the birthday girl to the bar, get her a drink, and we can talk more privately."

He holds out his elbow, and Lola is smart to scurry forward. Her action puts more space between Trent and Silas, possibly preventing a fight.

Silas starts to follow them, but Archer snags his elbow to pull him back.

"Unless you plan on making things right with Lola this minute, sit your ass down," Archer grinds out. "You just humiliated the girl in front of everyone on her fucking birthday. Don't do it a second time."

"Let him get her a drink while you think about your weird asshole actions," Georgia chimes in.

Silas slumps down into his chair. A man who always exudes confidence appears as if he took a beatdown.

"What the hell was that about?" Cohen asks. "Why would you do that shit to Lola?"

Even though they're friends who respect the bro code, they have no problem calling each other out when they're in the wrong.

"I'm so confused," I mutter.

"We all are," Cassidy says, not bothering to lower her voice so Silas doesn't hear. "Lola was looking at Silas with stars and horniness in her eyes. Instead of nicely turning her down, he pushed her off his lap." She shakes her head. "That has to do something to a girl's ego. Especially when Silas acts like he's in love with her."

"Acts like?" Finn snorts. "Silas *is* in love with her."

"I hate that motherfucker," Silas says out of nowhere. "I'm doing everything not to storm down there and beat his ass."

"Why do you hate him?" Jamie asks softly.

Silas taps his foot. "He's shady as fuck."

"He's shady as fuck because he's really shady as fuck or he's shady as fuck because he's flirting with Lola?" Lincoln asks.

"Both." Silas grimaces.

"Are you going to finally admit you two have hooked up?" Georgia asks, always one to ask for gossip.

Silas stares at his tapping foot. "Nah, we've never had sex."

"But have you *hooked up*?" Sierra clarifies.

Silas stays quiet.

"How about this?" Finn says. "Grow some balls and go apologize and tell Lola how you feel."

Silas's eyes are sharp when he stares at Finn. "I could say the same shit to you, brother."

I freeze.

Finn hunches forward. "Don't take your anger out on me, man."

Silas points at me. "Grace wouldn't be pregnant with another man's baby had you grown some balls."

I jerk my head back. As I clutch my stomach, my heartbeat turns sluggish. My thoughts cloud as if I'd drunk as much as Lola.

Silas has never acted like this before.

Finn jumps to his feet and bares his teeth. "Watch your goddamn mouth."

"Does the truth hurt?" Silas asks, his stare on Finn intense.

They're in a standoff, only inches apart, while everyone gawks at them. Within seconds, Archer is back on his feet, prepared to intervene in yet another altercation.

Finn wipes the edge of his mouth, and his tone turns more scathing. "Like you're doing with Lola? Instead, she's going to hook up with your stepbrother."

Silas rears his fist back, but Archer stops him.

"Whoa," Georgia says. "We all know Lola isn't hooking up with anyone tonight."

I grip Finn's wrist, not only to stop him but also for assistance to stand. "This is not the place. Let's go."

Silas pays a glance at me, and his face drops as if he sees the humiliation on mine. "Shit, Grace. I'm sorry." Regret ripples through his eyes. "I was pissed and—"

"It's fine." I run my hands up and down my arms. "I just ..." I'm holding in tears. "It's time for us to go."

Silas folds his hands together and bows his head. "Really, Grace—"

I stop him again. "You're sorry. Okay. I get it."

If we don't leave in a minute, I'm going to break down.

Without another word, Silas turns and storms off.

Finn grips my hand tighter than he ever has. "Someone, go talk to Silas because it damn sure won't be me tonight. We'll talk to you guys later."

People hug me good-bye, telling me not to take Silas's words to heart. The mood is somber. Something like this has never happened in our group. Sure, there are disagreements. Georgia and Archer hated each other for months, but nothing like this.

Even though our friends have joked about Finn and me liking each other, it's always been done in humor.

Never in anger.

Never has it sounded so bold and in our faces.

It was a verbal smack of truth straight to the heart.

Silas was right. If Finn *and I*—not just him—had stopped being scared, maybe I wouldn't be pregnant with another man's baby. Even with the pregnancy, even with us faking it, still, neither one of us has told each other our true feelings.

Our steps are rushed as we leave the club.

As I sit in his passenger seat, I open my mouth ... then shut it ... then open it. No words come to me—except for Silas's that keep running through my mind. Finn tightly grips the steering wheel and is focused on the road. It's a quiet ride, the only sound the pop station playing quietly on the radio.

"I'm sorry," I whisper into the darkness of the car when he parks in the driveway.

Even though I'm unsure of what exactly I'm apologizing for, I'm sorry for a multitude of things.

Not opening up my heart to Finn when I should've.

Getting pregnant by Gavin.

Asking Finn to sacrifice so much because of a decision I made.

Not telling off Silas for his hurtful words.

There's so much I wish I could take back.

I play with the strap of my bag. "Obviously, Silas was in the wrong for what he said—"

"Nah," Finn interrupts, resentment in his tone. "Silas was right."

"What?" I sputter, freezing.

"He was a dick about it—that's for sure. But that doesn't mean he was wrong." He shuts off the car and jerks the keys out. "I should've told you my feelings years ago."

My breathing restricts as tingles rush up my chest. "What are you talking about?"

He shifts to face me, and I wish the darkness didn't block out his face. "I'm talking about how I've been too chickenshit to admit that my heart beats for you, Grace. That it nearly broke me when I found out you were pregnant ... and it wasn't with my baby."

Silence fills the car as I digest what he just said.

Take in every word of his confession.

Words I've wanted to hear for so long, but it almost feels like it's too late now.

# CHAPTER TWENTY-ONE

# *Finn*

THIS MIGHT NOT BE the ideal place to finally confess my feelings, but it needed to be said. Holding it in for so long had been a mistake.

Grace getting pregnant should've been a hard enough smack in the face, but I was stupid. What shoved me over the line? Seeing the heartache on Silas's face when Lola walked off with Trent. Another push in the right direction was Silas setting my ass straight. His words were harsh but much needed. It was time I stopped pretending, or I'd be the next man watching the woman he loved leave with another man.

It might be too late to change Grace being pregnant, but I can change her not being mine.

Grace is quiet.

*Is her silence good? Bad?*

*Did my honesty scare her?*

"Want to go inside?" I unsnap my seat belt. "I hate not being able to see you."

Turning on the overhead light is an option but still not enough. I want to see every expression that crosses Grace's face when I lay out my truths to her.

"Yes," she whispers into the darkness. "Let's go inside."

I gulp a mouthful of air before stepping out of my car. Grace does the same, and we meet where her walkway starts. I rest my palm on the curve of her back as we walk up the porch steps and into the house. The door clicks behind us, and I follow her into the living room, flipping on the lights.

Grace turns and focuses her eyes on me in expectation. There's no going back now. I can't say what I said and then chicken out. I zero in on her, admiring how beautiful the woman I'm in love with is. Her strawberry-blond hair is in some type of French twist, exposing her radiant face. A light-pink shimmer is glossed over her lips, making me want to taste it.

Grace is everything I want but what I don't deserve.

That's what my head has always told me.

I was stupid for listening to it.

*Why did I think I don't deserve her?*

I don't come from money. Grace gives no fucks about that.

I don't have a fancy-ass college degree. Grace has never judged me for it.

I don't come from her world. Grace has never said she wants differently.

Not once has Grace given me a reason to believe I'm not good enough for her, so why am I holding myself back? I'm tired of being scared—because I am good enough, damn it.

I'm a good man who's taken care of himself when no one else would.

I'm a helping hand to anyone, even those who don't deserve it.

When the day comes, I'll do anything for Grace's baby.

"Grace." My voice hitches with emotion when I say her name.

I advance a step, bringing myself closer to her. She needs to see the honesty in my eyes—a testament that she's everything

I'll ever want. I can hear my heart thrumming in my chest from the combination of my fear and excitement.

I'm going to spill my heart out to her.

This could result in rejection.

A lost friendship.

But it needs to be done.

If Grace turns me down, I'll still be her friend.

Still be a call away for anything she needs.

We make eye contact, and I scramble for the right words.

*I can't fuck this up.*

Grace stares at me, unsure of where I'm going with this.

If I'll say what I need to say.

Hell, I'm playing this by ear.

Thirty minutes ago, I was sitting in a club, having no idea this would happen.

Reaching out, I cup her face with both my hands. "I'm in love with you."

I don't want to waste time with bullshit words.

I'm not good with them.

Knowing me, I'd fuck them up.

What's a better way to explain yourself to someone than to say those words?

*I love you.*

It says so much.

She squints at me, fluttering her eyelashes while processing what I said.

"What?" Her voice is shaky.

My body relaxes as I repeat myself, "I'm in love with you."

I stroke her cheek with my thumb.

My truth is finally released.

Her chin trembles underneath my hands. "I love you too, Finn."

I'd dreamed about this moment happening countless times. It went differently. The excitement I'd hoped for was nonexistent. She said the words I'd been dying to hear, but they were said with the enthusiasm of someone finding out their vacation had been canceled.

There's no excitement.

Yet it's also not rejection.

It's ... indifference?

My throat constricts, and I pull away as if my touch were no longer welcome. The heaviness of reality consumes me.

Grace winces, her eyes squeezing shut at the loss of me. "I'm sure this isn't the reaction you expected."

I step back. "I'm not sure what I expected."

Her eyes are watery when she opens them. "Finn," she says my name as if it pains her. "This has everything to do with me and nothing to do with you."

The high I felt for vomiting out my truth crumbles.

I rub my chin with one hand. "I think us admitting we're in love with each other has something to do with me."

Her face is expressionless. "If this were months ago, it'd be different."

"How?"

"I'm pregnant!" she shrieks, gesturing to her belly. "With another man's baby. That changes everything."

"You think I give a shit about that?" I rush out before allowing myself to polish my response. I pound my hand against my chest. "That changes nothing. I don't love you any less. I'm telling you I love you as you are—*everything* you are. I'm done playing pretend. I want this"—I indicate between us —"to be real. I want to spend the rest of my life with you."

She gawks at me, her mouth hanging open.

I lose a breath when she steps closer, stands on her tiptoes, and presses her lips against mine.

Everything happens so fast.

I curl my arm around her waist and drag her close.

Now that I have her, I'm never letting her go.

"Grace," I whisper against her soft lips, "you have no idea how long I've wanted this. To be able to do this."

It's my turn to kiss her.

Our kiss starts out impulsive.

It turns hot.

Hungry.

Desperate.

I slip my tongue between her lips and into her mouth, and the taste of strawberry lip gloss hits me. Grace sighs as our lips caress each other's. Our mouths stay connected as I walk us to the couch. I fall back onto it and pull her onto my lap. My dick immediately hardens when she straddles me. I grip her hips and bite into her lower lip before raining kisses down her jaw and neck.

Goose bumps pop up along her soft skin in the wake of my lips. My excitement explodes when she shudders at my touch. Bunching up her dress to her hips, I shove my hands underneath it, no longer able to hold back the urge to touch her.

To touch her the ways I've wanted to for years.

She rocks against me and whispers, "More."

My eyes widen, as I'm momentarily shocked, and I give her what she wants.

*More.*

Using a single finger, I slip her panties to the side and dip my finger inside.

"Shit, baby," I hiss. "You're soaked."

"For you," she says, encircling her arms around my neck. "Just for you."

To help me, she tilts her waist back, and I slide my finger between her folds.

I've never been so turned on in my life.

She writhes above me and gasps when I thrust a finger inside her.

Her pussy is a tight wall against my single finger.

*Will she be comfortable taking my cock?*

I halt, stopping myself at the thought.

I'm going too fast.

She loses a breath and stares at me, wide-eyed, when I slowly draw my finger out of her. My chest heaves in and out, and I drop my head back, resting it against the cushion.

"Shit, Grace," I groan. "I'm sorry."

"Why are you sorry?" she slowly asks. "Why'd you stop?"

I raise my head to meet her gaze. "I don't want to rush this with you. I didn't tell you I loved you to sleep with you."

She needs to know my intentions for baring myself to her wasn't to have sex.

I rest my hand on her shaky thigh.

"Is it because I'm pregnant?"

Her question shocks me into silence.

I've never slept with a pregnant woman before. Not because I find them unattractive. But this is Grace. I want her any way I can have her.

Before I can say she's lost her mind and her pregnancy has nothing to do with me stopping us, she whispers, "I know I'm bigger. A pregnant body might not exactly be a turn-on ... especially with it not being your baby."

My chest seizes tight. I hate when she points that out.

"I understand, Finn," she adds in a strained voice.

"What?" I pull back and stare at her, stunned, and soften my voice. "Baby, my attraction to you is not the issue. It will *never* be the issue." I tilt my hips up, grinding my erection between her thighs. "Feel how hard my cock is for you? I just don't want to rush it."

"But—"

I press my finger against her lips. "Let me prove it to you." I grind against her again. "Show you how much I've wanted to have you for years. How I've wanted to take you, all cute and polite, and dirty you up in bed. You have no idea how bad I've wanted to make you mine, fuck you the way I know you should be fucked, and never let you go."

My voice is raspy after my confession.

Some words I meant to say.

Some I didn't.

Maybe she wasn't ready to hear all that yet.

"Do it," she says, challenging me. "Make me yours. Prove you want me like this."

Pushing my hands between us, I tighten my hold on her ass to lift her. She wraps her legs around my waist as I stand and head to her bedroom. As hot as messing around on the couch sounds, I want her in a bed. I need ample room to show her she's everything to me.

I flip the light on, carefully set her on her feet, and sit on the edge of the bed. I drink her in as she stares at me in curiosity.

Crossing my arms, I lower my voice. "Strip for me. Show me that gorgeous body I've lusted over for years."

# CHAPTER TWENTY-TWO

# Grace

FINN'S WORDS light a fire inside me.

I'm a vanilla girl.

I've only had sex with vanilla men.

*Straight to missionary* type of men.

I'd bet my car Finn isn't a vanilla, *straight to missionary* man.

A man asking me to strip is new.

If it were any other man asking, I'd be timid.

Uncertain.

But this is Finn.

And the way he's eyeing me like a snack gives me a boost of confidence.

*He wants me to strip for him?*

I'll strip for him.

My breathing is ragged as I step out of my dress. Without thinking, I wrap my hands around my stomach, hiding myself.

"All of you, Grace," Finn demands. "Every single inch."

I drop my arms, unsnap my bra, and my breasts burst free.

"Shit," he mutters.

I stand tall, wearing only panties, a sense of pride shooting through my veins. I don't bother covering my breasts because I know his next command would've told me not to. Finn licks his lips, his stare sweeping up and down my body in appreciation.

"You are the sexiest woman I've ever seen." He falls back onto his elbows, holding himself up. "Now, let me see that pretty pussy of yours."

I nearly fall back a step at his words.

I rub my thighs together, feeling the stickiness of my arousal, and run a finger between my legs before slowly pushing my panties down.

"You're soaked for me, aren't you?" he croaks out.

I smirk. "Possibly."

*Two can play this teasing game, buddy.*

My eyes sweep straight to him as my panties fall to the carpet, and I kick them off my feet.

He rises, no longer on his elbows, and his back is straight. "And you thought I wouldn't find this the sexiest damn thing ever?" His breathing turns ragged. "You are breathtakingly beautiful." He crooks his finger, signaling for me to come closer.

I erase the distance between us, and he raises my leg onto the bed. I shudder as he strokes the inside of my thigh.

"I love this body of yours"—he plants a soft kiss to my growing belly—"every inch of you, and I'm going to show that appreciation by worshipping your pussy." He widens the space between my legs, dragging his hand up and down my thigh. "Can I taste you, Grace?"

"Yes," I half gasp, half moan.

"That's my girl."

Standing, he carefully pushes me onto the bed and climbs over me. I relax into my mattress, ready for whatever he's willing to give me. Goose bumps coat my skin when he slips a hand up my thigh before settling himself between my ankles.

He spreads my legs wide, putting me on full display for him.

Another first time for me.

Call it the pregnancy hormones.

Call it being with Finn.

But for the first time in my years of having sex, I've never felt so comfortable with someone.

Finn lowers his head and stares between my legs, as if he were studying for a test. His head falls forward, and he takes my clit between his lips, gently sucking on it. "I'm going to make you feel so good, baby."

"Oh my God," I mutter, tingles shooting up my spine.

With no warning, he dips his head lower and strokes the length of his tongue between my lower lips. My back hitches off the bed as a burst of pleasure shatters through me.

It's only the first lick, and I'm already a goner.

I grip the back of his neck, holding him down. "More, please."

He chuckles. "Oh, I'm going to have fun with you."

I grin.

*No more vanilla sex for this girl.*

Finn is awakening sexual urges I've never had before.

I've never been a fan of oral sex because it's never been a fun time. It's an annoying attempt where men fake making an effort to make you orgasm but never actually reach the finish line.

Finn?

He's putting in all the effort.

He gets an A+++++ for the things he's doing with his tongue.

He adds his fingers.

Sucks on my clit.

I writhe on the sheets and moan his name.

The same way I have when I've fingered myself, thinking about him, but this is so much better than anything I could've ever imagined. I move into his touch, grinding my core against his face, and I'm shocked he's not gasping for air at how tight

I'm holding him. I want him there forever. A warm wave of pleasure hits me, shooting through my veins and lighting me on fire.

Finn groans against my clit as I ride out the wave of my orgasm.

My Finn-induced orgasm.

The best damn orgasm of my life.

"Holy freaking crap," I gasp. "I'm going to ask you if you think I'm attractive every day if that's what you do to prove me otherwise." I'm not sure how much he understands since I'm saying the words through heavy puffs of air.

He chuckles—it's deep and raw. He pulls back and swipes his tongue over his wet lips—wet from my getting off on his face. I expect his next steps to be rolling off the bed, scurrying to the bathroom, and rinsing out his mouth.

That move was a Gavin regular.

I should've known Finn is nothing like Gavin.

I love the feel of his body weight as he moves up my body and slaps a kiss to my lips.

He lingers for a moment, sliding his tongue between my lips. "Don't you taste good?"

I'm not exactly sure what *good* vagina tastes like, and I can't taste much, so I nod and mutter, "Mm-hmm."

He collapses onto his back and catches his breath. "That is definitely a top ten best moment of my life."

"Oh, really?" I turn on my side and prop myself up with my elbow. Looking down, I meet his eyes. They're tired but lust-filled. "What's number one on that list?"

Without one moment of hesitation, he answers, "Hearing you say you love me."

I didn't expect that.

Sure, other men have said they loved me.

But not for a second do I doubt Finn's love for me.

This is the moment I realize that even though I've said

those words to other men, I've never meant them. My heart had never filled with so much emotion like it did with Finn when those three words slipped past my lips.

I stare down at him with half-lidded eyes. "That's mine too."

He grins and taps his fingers along his lips.

I slide closer to him, and he clutches the back of my neck to bring me closer. Our kiss is slow, sensual, and when I pull back, something catches my eyes.

Finn's erection underneath his jeans.

My mouth waters, wanting to taste him just as bad as he did me.

"Can I add another top ten to mine?"

He raises a brow at the same time I climb over him.

I seat myself at his knees and run my hand along the outline of his cock. "Let me return the favor."

He groans as I take both hands and slide them up and down each side of his dick.

Excitement zips through me.

Like with men performing oral on me, I've never been a fan of sucking cock before.

At this moment, there's nothing more I want than to see Finn take his dick out and feed it between my lips.

"I want to taste you," I say, practically begging.

Finn starts to rise. "Grace, you don't have to."

I lean forward, remembering I'm naked for the first time as my boobs rub against the roughness of his jeans. "I *want* to." Smiling, I press my palm to his chest and shove him down.

I hate that my hands shake as I unbuckle his jeans. It's not that I'm nervous or that I don't want to. I'm excited that this is finally happening. I want to see all of Finn and show him I can pleasure him just as good as he pleasures me.

*Well, I don't think my skills will ever match up to his.*

The man has a talented tongue.

Finn tilts up his hips, helping me push down his jeans. I

don't bother pulling them all the way off, and they stay bunched up around his ankles.

His cock stands at full attention. It's bigger than I anticipated, bigger than any cock I've seen. That's even including the porn Lola sent me the links to when I was in a dry spell. Since I teach my students measurements, I know he's *at least* a good six inches.

The man's cock is half a darn full ruler size.

I gulp, unsure of how well I can take in his length.

Finn grips the bottom of his cock. "Do whatever you feel comfortable with, babe. I don't expect you to deep-throat, swallow, whatever. This cock is yours to do with as you please."

I clasp my hand over his. "I want to do what you like. Show me."

He slips his hand off his cock before covering mine with it. With his eyes on me, he waits until I meet his stare before using both our hands to jerk him off. When we reach the head, he twists our hands, and we lose eye contact as he drops his head back and groans.

"You good on your own?" he rasps out.

I nod.

His hand disappears, leaving me on my own, and Finn props himself up onto his elbows, giving himself a perfect view of me about to suck his cock. I do one last stroke before lowering my head and licking the tip.

"Yes," he groans.

I open my mouth wide, and in my head, I replay the porn I watched, remembering how the woman hollowed her cheeks out as she sucked. My lips curl around his cock as I give him the best blow job I've ever given in my life. Slobber slides down my lips and onto my chin, hitting the sheets.

"Grace," Finn moans. "Just like that, baby."

His hand goes to my head the same way I did with him— only he's gentle, slowly guiding me into sucking him just as he likes it. Lowering my hand, I play with his balls, squeezing them. His knees lock up, tightening the room I have between them.

"I'm coming," he warns, grabbing the base of his dick as if ready to stop it while waiting for my reaction.

"In my mouth," I say against his cock, unsure whether he can understand me. To be clear, I give him a thumbs-up, and he chuckles at the same time his cum spurts into my mouth.

Finn relaxes against the sheets. "And that's made it to the top ten list."

I laugh, a red blush creeping up my cheeks.

I'm a bit shy but also proud of myself.

*I did that. I made him come that hard.*

After we catch our breaths, Finn kisses me softly before helping me out of bed. He scurries to his bathroom while I brush my teeth. As I'm finishing up, he joins me in the bathroom, and nervousness hits me.

*Is he sleeping with me tonight?*

I don't want to assume something, but surely, if a man had his face between my legs, he'd at least want to stay to sleep off the exhaustion of pleasuring me?

I want him in my bed.

To stay with me tonight ... and every night.

As I'm lost in thought, Finn comes up behind me and circles his arms around my waist.

"Can I stay with you tonight?" he softly asks in my ear.

I reach up and clutch the top of his arm. "Yes, and you never have to question the answer to that again."

As I snuggle into his arms, I sleep through the night.

No nightmares.

Only a dream ... of Finn being with me forever, of him being a father figure to my child, and of us having more children.

"I DON'T KNOW how I'm supposed to see my friends with a straight face."

Finn and I are standing in the kitchen. I'm drinking orange juice and him coffee. Even though we crossed friendship lines last night, it hasn't been awkward this morning. It's comfortable, as if waking up in each other's arms was what our future had been destined to be.

Finn winks at me. "Why's that?" The smirk on his face confirms he knows exactly why.

I bring my cup to my lips, smiling and speaking inside it, "You gave me the best orgasm of my life. I'm going to be walking around with orgasmed-out stars in my eyes for the next month."

He stands taller, pride on his face. "Let's not forget your skills either." He whistles. "I struggled not to come in seconds."

Pride settles through me at the compliment of pleasuring him like that. I've never felt so sexy, so skilled, as Finn makes me. Never has a man made me feel more attractive—with the weight gain, pregnant belly, and all.

I set my cup on the counter and swallow, remembering how he tasted inside my mouth. It's something I want to have over and over again. I read that pregnant women are horny a lot, but I've never wanted to taste, to kiss, to be with a man as badly as I do with Finn.

"Those words aren't going to help me keep a straight face, mister." I wiggle my finger in his direction.

He leans against the counter with his legs slightly open. "All you have to do is spend the morning questioning Lola about her and Silas."

"Lola won't mutter a word about it. You know how private she is."

"You find anything out, you share the gossip."

I shake my head. "If she says not to, I can't break girl code."

He places his hand to his chest and gasps. "Not even for ..." He briefly pauses and furrows his brows. "Your guy best friend?"

I frown. "Is that what you are still? My guy best friend?"

He fixes his deep stare on me. "I'd love to say boyfriend, but I don't want to assume anything. I'm afraid of jumping too fast and scaring you, Grace."

"Us together doesn't scare me." My words are rushed out.

"You want to be mine then?" He strokes his jaw while waiting for my answer.

"I want to be your everything."

He narrows the gap between us, grips my waist, and lifts me onto the counter. "You've been my everything for years."

***

"FIRST THINGS FIRST," Georgia announces when the waitress returns with our drink orders—lemonade for Cassidy and me and mimosas for everyone else. "Lola, we need to know what the hell happened last night."

It's a tradition for us girls to go out for our birthdays and then do a brunch the day after. Brunch is where we hand over gifts and gossip. Lola chose a small bistro that makes the best sandwiches, and the weather is nice enough for us to sit outside. Not too hot, yet not too cold. We're seated around a table, ready for food and gossip.

Lola, sporting oversize black sunglasses, shakes her head. "First things first. I'm hungover, and I'll talk about anything but that."

"Come on," Georgia says, the only one having the guts to question Lola. "What pissed off Silas so much that he acted how he did?"

Since Cassidy and Jamie are new to the group, they don't

push the friendship boundaries as much as Georgia does with everyone. For some reason, my short, sarcastic friend can pull the truth out of anyone. Although Lola is a tough nut to crack.

"I've never seen him like that," I add. "He threw you off his lap."

I'm certain my comment will cause Lola to come to Silas's defense. Even with whatever happened to them last night, she's always his biggest supporter.

Lola snatches her mimosa. She wraps her fingers around the glass, her long black nails on display. "Silas doesn't like it when I drink that much." She shrugs as if we'd believe her half-assed answer.

"There's no way he was that mad over you having a few drinks," Georgia deadpans next to her. "Not to mention, you looked like you wanted to jump his bones."

"It was actually hot," Cassidy inputs. "Until the whole dropping you on your ass part."

Lola winces at the reminder. "Sorry, but I'd prefer not to talk about my best friend rejecting me. It was dumb on my part, smart on his."

Silas and Lola are two of a kind. They share a *give no fucks* attitude and are fun. We'll give last night a *get-out-of-jail-free* card for their bizarre behavior. We all insist they hook up on the down-low, but they deny it. Last night makes me rethink that notion.

"What about his stepbrother?" Jamie asks, letting Lola off the hook. "You two looked chummy."

Lola sighs dramatically. "He's nice. We exchanged numbers. He walked me to Lincoln's car, where he and Cass took my drunken ass home." She throws Cassidy an appreciative nod.

"He was a gentleman," Cassidy adds. "With how Silas described him, I expected him to be a jackass. While we waited for Lincoln's car, he chatted with us. I think Silas was jealous of him buying Lola a drink."

"Is it weird, though?" I ask, hoping I don't sound like a Debbie Downer. "With him being Silas's stepbrother?"

Lola licks her red lips. "They're not close. Their parents didn't start dating until their senior year of high school, and they never hung out. Silas's mother left his father for Trent's dad. I understand Silas not being a fan, but Trent had nothing to do with what his dad did. According to Trent, Silas has hated him since the day they met."

"As bad as it sounds, I get his anger," Sierra says. "I was pissed when I found out my father had an affair and secret child. I took it out on my brother's girlfriend for a while since she had something to do with it."

Lola nods. "My father was the king of affairs. It's why I don't trust men."

"Since Lola won't share anything, let's move on to Grace and Finn," Georgia says, causing everyone's attention to flash to me. "Finn looked ready to kill Silas for what he said about you getting pregnant because Finn was a wuss."

My straw squeaks as I move it in and out of my cup. "I'm happy he did. It knocked sense into Finn." A smile spreads across my lips at thoughts of being with Finn last night.

On my drive to brunch, I devised different stories to explain how our night went. With all of Lola's drama, I wasn't sure if Finn and I would come up. I should've known if Lola stayed quiet, I'd be the next in line.

Georgia gapes at me. "What?"

"Now, this is a much better conversation." Lola leans back in her chair and sucks on the orange from her drink. "Did you fuck?" She's never one ot beat around the bush or worry about her words.

I play with my hands in my lap. "We didn't ... have sex. Just messed around."

"First base?" Georgia asks. "Second base?"

A collection of amused stares is pinned on me.

"What base is tongues?" I relax in my chair.

It's a relief to finally say that Finn and I share the same feelings out loud. These are my friends, and they'd never judge me. There isn't one person at the table who doesn't show a sign of excitement. Even Lola's hungover ass is grinning.

"How was it?" Cassidy asks.

My smile is so wide that my teeth are showing. "It was amazing. I could spend the rest of my life having him ... go downtown on me."

"Cheers to that!" Georgia says.

Everyone raises their glasses and clinks them against each other's.

"Does that mean you're dating now?" Sierra asks.

"I don't know." My shoulder slump, and I lose the grin I've worn all day. "His feelings for me might change after the baby is born. I'm going to get fat—"

"Shut the hell up with that attitude," Lola interrupts. "Finn worships you. He isn't going anywhere."

# CHAPTER TWENTY-THREE

# *Finn*

AFTER GRACE LEAVES, I shower, grab the baby book from her nightstand, and stride into the kitchen to make myself a lunch. With a plated turkey sandwich in hand, I venture to the living room and make myself comfortable on the couch. Taking a bite, I start educating myself on all things pregnancy and baby. I want to be able to help Grace with whatever she needs.

I try to block out what'll happen when the baby is born. Before last night, I was sure I'd never be able to have her. Now? I have more hope of that not happening.

My baby education is interrupted when my phone chimes with a text.

**Silas: Can we talk?**

I expected him to reach out to me today. Silas is a good dude, and we've never had issues. His dickhead behavior last night was out of the ordinary.

**Me: If it's about last night, I get it.**

**Silas: Are you with Grace?**

**Me: Nah, she's at the birthday brunch.**

Seconds later, my phone rings.

Silas.

"I was an asshole last night," he says when I answer. "I wish I could blame it on the alcohol, but that's obviously not the case."

"Nah, dude." I set my sandwich down and transfer the plate to the coffee table. "I'm buying you dinner for helping me get my head out of my ass."

"Does that mean you finally told Grace how you feel?"

"Sure did," I reply with a nod.

"How'd that work out?" His tone is layered with confidence.

"Pretty damn good." I stretch out on the couch, a dopey smile on my face.

"I'm happy for you, man." He chuckles. "Looks like you do owe me dinner."

"Now, it's time for you and Lola to do the same." It's ballsy of me to bring up Lola after what happened last night. "You're the last couple in our group who needs to get their shit together."

Our group started out as individuals, and everyone has started coupling up.

"Lola and I are ... more complicated than Grace and you," he says irritably.

I shut my eyes, hating that I need to make this point to him. "Trent was hitting on her. You need to make your move before she gives him a chance."

He scoffs. "Lola isn't that fucking stupid."

I mock his scoff. "Do you remember what you did last night?"

Silence.

I can almost picture him grinding his jaw.

He needs to be hit with the truth.

"You dropped her on her ass on her birthday," I state. "She walked off with Trent. We both know it wasn't only a friendly gesture from Trent."

"I have to go. I'll talk to you later, man."

He ends the call.

AS BAD AS I hate not being at the bar, I'm beginning to enjoy my job at the dealership.

My bank account also likes it.

My coworkers are starting to come around, and there's a sense of deep pride every time I sell a car. I loved my job at the Twisted Fox, but it's almost like I hit an achievement each time someone thanks me for helping them get their dream ride.

Another plus?

The dealership is close to Grace's school, and our lunch breaks are at the same time.

"Hi, Finn!" A bright smile crosses over Rachelle's face when I enter the school's office. "You brought Grace and the baby lunch. So cute!"

The more Grace's belly grows, the more questions she gets. Me bringing her lunch regularly has led some of her coworkers, including Rachelle, to assume I'm the father. I have no problem with those assumptions. Like them though, I'm curious as to who the father is. Anytime the topic is brought up, Grace shuts down. She's already going through enough, so I'm scared to push her. There's also the deep pit in my stomach when I think of learning the truth. From the few details she's told me about him, I already want to kick the motherfucker's ass. If I find out who he is and run into him, it might cause issues.

"Another visit?"

My gaze moves from Rachelle to find Principal Asshole strolling toward me. He stops behind Rachelle, his fingers gripping the back of her chair, and icily stares at me. Thrusting out his chin, he crosses his arms.

I return his glare. The weird-ass motherfucker keeps creeping up every time I'm here as if he were watching the parking lot. I want to hop over the counter and ask what his problem is, but I can't. That could result in the end of lunch visits with Grace. I'm sure fighting the principal is a straight road to being banned from the school.

Holding up the bag of boxed chef salads, I smile. "Grace loves her Freddy's salads."

"I'm well aware," Asshole grits out.

*The fuck is that supposed to mean?*

His response rubs me the wrong way, but I act like it doesn't.

*Don't let him know his words affect you.*

Rachelle smiles again—this one not as genuine as before. "You know where her room is, Finn. Enjoy your lunch." She's catching on to his weird sudden appearances too.

"I suggest limiting your visits," Asshole says, glowering at me. "You're becoming a distraction to my female employees."

*Ah, there it is.*

Jealousy.

Not only that, but his creepy factor also keeps moving up notches.

*His female employees?*

Rachelle gasps, her face paling.

He curls his upper lip and glowers at Rachelle. "That includes you."

Not wanting this to go further, I turn and shake my head.

"You're one weird-ass dude," I mutter under my breath. Without waiting to find out if he heard me, I yank the door open and leave the office.

The scent of cafeteria food is in the air, and a kid yells, "Hey! I'm the line leader," before shoving another away.

Grace's classroom is at the end of the hall, and I tuck the bag of food underneath my elbow as I approach it. The door is open, and I tap my knuckle against it, lightly knocking.

Grace is standing on a chair, taping a poster to the wall. When each corner is secured, she turns to look at me from over her shoulder.

"Hey," she greets, sliding the tape into her pocket.

Advancing into her classroom, I drop our food and drinks onto a desk and help her down from the chair.

"You need to be careful doing that," I say, squeezing her hand tight before releasing it and smacking a kiss to her lips. "Don't they have ladders for that here?"

She pulls the tape from her pocket and drops it into her desk drawer. "Yes, but I hate hunting them down. A chair does just as good of a job."

"Did something happen between you and the principal?"

I curse myself for asking that so soon. I planned to approach the conversation while we ate, throwing it out there as small talk.

Grace lowers her gaze, her tone turning flustered. "Why ... why do you ask?"

"The way he reacts to seeing me isn't ..." I search for the right word to use without sounding too much like a dick. "It's not normal."

*Jealousy.*

That's what the man exudes whenever he sees me.

"Uh ..." Grace bites into her lower lip. "Kind of."

"Is he ...?" I stop, allowing my words to trail off, unable to say them out loud.

"He is," she says, her voice quiet and shaky.

My chest tightens. I turn my head to the side and tightly shut my eyes, digesting the news. "Oh, wow." It takes a moment before my stare returns to her. "I guess that finally answers the question of who the father is."

"It does," Grace whispers, her hands clutching her stomach. "Unfortunately."

"Fucking asshole." I grit my teeth and want to throw the food across the room. "I want to beat his ass."

My mind scrambles with what Grace told me about him being married and keeping it from her. *What a dumbass.*

"Trust me." She cringes. "I want to kick his ass every day I see him."

"Wow." I slide onto a student's chair, the connected desk tight at my stomach. "It's going to be hard not to kill him when I'm here."

This new revelation won't stop me from visiting Grace.

I was worried about being a dick before, but now that I know what he did to Grace, there's no more Mr. Nice Guy. If he says something smart, I might not be able to touch him with my hands, but I'll give him a verbal beatdown like no other. He'll know never to mess with Grace.

"Look on the bright side," Grace says. "Had he not done what he did, maybe we wouldn't be together like we are now."

"Or maybe you wouldn't be pregnant by the cheating dick. Eventually, we would've dragged our heads out of our asses."

Grace flinches at my response, all the color draining from her face.

"Shit, sorry." I roughly drag a hand through my hair, tugging at the ends to cause myself pain—an attempt to forget about Principal Asshole. I can't let my anger get the best of me in front of Grace. It'll only make her feel worse about the situation.

I snatch the bag from the desk and start dragging out the contents. My appetite is gone, and the sight of the food makes my stomach curl. I snap off the lid and hand Grace's salad to her. I don't even bother with mine. I gesture to her to sit down, and she warily does.

"How did it start between you and him?" I ask, standing in front of her desk.

Grace unwraps a plastic fork. "Having this conversation while in the same building as him isn't a good idea."

I snap my fingers. "Good point. Speaking of being in the same building, you think you can do this every day? What about when you have the baby?"

"I don't love being around him, but I also won't give him the satisfaction of pushing me out of my job. I was here first." She grabs her drink and uses it to point to the door. "He can go."

"If he messes with you, tell me. Tell someone. It seems he doesn't like the idea of you being with anyone else."

That's an understatement. Dude goes into creep mode.

"It's because he still wants to be with me." She drops her fork at her confession—a sign that she didn't plan on disclosing that information.

I raise a brow, and my lungs constrict. "What?"

"He wants me to wait for him until he can leave his wife."

"Are you ...?" I glance at the door, watching it as if he'll appear there. "You're not considering that, are you?"

"What?" she shrieks. "Absolutely not. I want to be with you, Finn. *Only you.*"

I swear, when I take another glance at the door, someone scurries away from it.

---

"DO ME A FAVOR?" I slide out a barstool and plop down on it.

Since it's early, Silas is the only one working the bar. Not many people go for a drink straight after work. It's something I've never done. I used to work until the wee hours of the morning, and the act always reminded me of my father.

When he actually held a job, he'd reward himself with a drink—well, *drinks*—afterward.

Silas wipes his hands with a rag while strolling over to me and throws it over his shoulder. "Yeah?"

I wrap my feet around the stool legs, already feeling dizzy before drinking an ounce of liquor. "Pour me a drink."

He nods, smiling quizzically. "I got you."

Turning on his heels, he sings along with the music playing in the background. He chooses a bottle of vodka—the most expensive one Twisted Fox carries—and pours me a double.

Grace had plans with Faith after work. Not wanting to be alone, I drove to Twisted Fox. A drink will help clear my head. It was difficult, focusing on work after discovering Grace works with the guy who knocked her up. Not only that but he also wants to be with her. I shudder at the thought of her falling victim to his games again. Grace is strong, but the guy sounds like a master manipulator. It'd kill me to lose Grace to him.

He could leave his wife and ask Grace to be one big, happy family.

I finally have all I want in my hands, and today proved how easy it can slip away.

"You look like shit," Silas says, smacking a square napkin in front of me and setting my drink on top of it.

"I feel like shit." I knock back the vodka, and it burns down my throat.

He cocks his head. "What's up?"

"I met the guy who got Grace pregnant." Even after the vodka, my throat goes dry.

"Oh fuck. Who?"

I tap my fingers along my chin.

*Does anyone else know who the dad is?*

*Will that break our trust?*

Just like Silas won't tell us anything about him and Lola, if I confide in him about Grace, he'll remain tight-lipped.

"It's a guy who works at the school," I reply, pinching the bridge of my nose.

Silas studies me for a moment. "You've been thinking about them being around each other almost daily?"

"That ... among other things."

"Don't worry about it. Grace has been in love with you for years, man."

"Nothing is ever permanent, though." I sigh, hating that I'm being this negative man. "Even when there's love, relationships don't always work out."

I rest my elbows on the table. I came to the bar to chat with the bartender, like one of those drunks who lives at bars. Now that I've said the words out loud, I no longer want to talk about it.

"And you and Lola?" I ask. "Any updates on her and Trent?"

Silas presses his fist to his mouth as if settling himself down from those names being said together. "She hasn't said a word to me, but from what I heard, they exchanged numbers." He shakes his head. "Lola is talking with Trent. Grace works with an ex. And we thought being friends with girls we liked was gonna be easy."

# CHAPTER TWENTY-FOUR

# Grace

"I WENT ON A DATE WITH TRENT," Lola tells Georgia and me.

"What?" I shriek. "How could you do that to Silas?"

Lola's face tightens, and she sucks in what sounds like an irritated breath. "Do what to Silas? He made it clear how he felt for me on my birthday."

I'm not sure if Lola is talking to—*dating*—Trent to get back at Silas for his behavior at the club or if she genuinely likes him. We're all best friends who share secrets, but Lola is the private one of the group. She provides the bare minimum about her life. Our friends haven't gotten together since the club, so I haven't witnessed how Silas and Lola are now. When we texted earlier, she told me they were fine.

"Have you talked to him about it?" I might as well be the one who dives into questions. She can't get that mad at a pregnant woman.

Lola shakes her head. "Barely. He texted and apologized that night. I told him it was no big deal, and I was over it."

"But you're not over it," I deadpan.

"I'm definitely not over it." She rests her elbows on the

table, the bangles around her wrist making a noise as they hit the table. A painful expression crosses her features. "Maybe this is the end of Silas and me."

Her statement startles me. That's a big deal.

"Yeah, right," Georgia says, leaning back in her stool. "You and Silas are two peas in a pod."

Lola drums her nails along her glass. "He's been distant lately." She flips her ebony hair over her shoulder before hunching forward. Her head drops—an attempt to hide the hurt flashing along her face.

I cringe. Lola has saved me from uncomfortable conversations countless times. It's time I do the same for her.

"Finn knows who my baby daddy is," I cry out.

All *Lola and Silas* talk are overrun by my confession. During Lola's birthday brunch, I shared the mess that was my relationship with Gavin.

"He knows about Principal Jackass?" Georgia asks before snarling. "I can't stand that asshole."

"That makes two of us," I grumble. "He keeps saying he wants to be with me."

I haven't told Finn about the many visits Gavin has paid to my classroom to tell me he was leaving his wife so we could be together. I don't entertain the idea and always tell him I don't care. He could leave his wife tonight, and I'd still want nothing to do with him.

Once a cheater, always a cheater in my book.

People can change—I'm well aware. But this man hid an entire marriage and family from me. He talks about his wife as if he has no respect for her, which is further proven by the cheating. I'd never trust Gavin, and he disgusts me. I hate that I ever allowed him to touch me.

The only man I want in my life, in my baby's life, is Finn.

"YOU OKAY?" Finn asks from across the table. "Is it morning sickness? Should we add doughnuts to the list of shit that makes you nauseous?"

"God, no," I grumble, wiping frosting from the edge of my mouth. "Thou shall not take a pregnant woman's doughnuts unless they want a pregnant woman's foot up their ass."

Since moving in, Finn declared himself the master of breakfast. It was a meal he typically didn't have, so he's tried everything. He either makes me breakfast or takes me out. The breakfast process has been a lot of trial and error.

He made eggs. They made me nauseous.

Oatmeal? Baby isn't a fan.

Bacon? Good ole bacon? I ran to the bathroom and puked.

Meat and dairy have become a thing of my non-pregnant past.

Now, all I want are foods dipped in ranch or taco sauce. I'm shocked I haven't dipped this Long John into some ranch yet.

Even with my love of doughnuts, I'm surprised I'm not sick. Not because they're gross. Nor is it because the baby isn't a fan. It's because today is an exciting one.

No more will I say *the baby*.

It'll be *he* or *she*.

Today, I'll find out the sex of my baby.

There's always a rush of pent-up excitement when I think about it.

Nervous jitters—but good nervous jitters.

Then, that happiness balloon bursts.

It'll be a good day but also a lonely one.

I'll have no one next to me at the appointment to share the good news with. No one holding my hand as we stare at the screen with anticipation. I'll be solo, a single mother.

Today's news will change my life.

Faith offered to join me, but it's parents' day at Raven's school. I'd feel terrible if Faith missed that because of me. I haven't broken the news to my parents yet, so my mother tagging along isn't an option either. I could ask one of my friends, but they're busy. There's also a twinge of embarrassment for bringing your best friend with you. It's as if they'd immediately know no one else was in the picture.

I also haven't asked them because I've been trying to build up the nerve to ask the man sitting across from me.

I shouldn't be nervous. The man has had his tongue between my legs, and his cock has been in my mouth.

Why am I scared of asking him to come with me to a doctor's appointment?

Finn has spent every night in my bed since the night of Lola's birthday party. We've snuggled, made out, and progressed to third base, but we haven't slept together yet. The first time we hooked up, we were a mix of emotions, of desire and lust. Now, it's as if one of us is afraid of crossing that line. When it comes, there'll be no going back. Sex is more final, and ever since I became pregnant, I've seen it as more of something that you only do out of love.

I shove the last bite of doughnut into my mouth and wash it down with apple juice. Not a good combination, but my pregnant appetite would have apple juice with every meal if possible.

"I, uh ..." I struggle to find the right words.

Finn sets his coffee to the side to provide me his full attention.

"Whatever it is, hit me." He rubs his hands together.

"I have a doctor's appointment today." I stare at him, unfocused, not wanting to see him as clearly in case he turns me down. "I'm going to find out the sex of the baby."

"Who's going with you?" His face hardens when I shake my head. "No one?"

I gulp. "No one."

"Wrong." He leans in close. "I'm going with you." He quickly presses a kiss to the tip of my nose.

That's the thing with Finn.

If he knows someone needs something, he's there.

Yes, we might be dating, but that doesn't mean he's obligated to go. He could've easily blamed it on work, especially since it'll be last minute.

With no hesitation, Finn said he'd be there.

Another event where Finn steps up and does Gavin's job.

Another action that'll pull me closer to him even though I know in the end, he'll leave. Finn is a thirty-year-old man who's never talked positively about commitment. When baby talk comes up with our friends, he always shakes his head and says he doesn't think it's for him.

*Does that mean my baby and I won't be for him either?*

It's one thing to hang out with the pregnant girl and another when there's a screaming newborn in the next room.

# CHAPTER TWENTY-FIVE

## Finn

RIGHT NOW, I'm like a damn toddler on Christmas morning.

Not that I've ever believed in Santa.

When I was at the old age of five, my father told me Santa was fake and wanted to make it clear that any gift I received was from him, period. Dick wanted to take all the credit ... even for the ones I received from different charity organizations.

I've been brimming in excitement all day. Hell, I'm shocked I haven't broken out in dance. For what seems like the hundredth time today, I check my watch. As soon as the time that I've been waiting for hits, I jump up from my chair.

I high-five Brian before leaving and getting in my car to pick up Grace for her appointment.

Today will be another addition to my top ten list.

Grace asked me to be there with her for this appointment. She's handing over a trust not easily given. She could've asked one of the girls to accompany her, but I was her pick. That feels damn good.

I blare my music, singing along with the song, and drive to Grace's school. When I pull into the parking lot, I spot her standing at the entrance. Her attention is on the children running around the playground. As I get closer, she turns, and her face practically glows when her eyes meet mine. I grin, and my heart fucking brightens at the reminder of where we're going.

The fact I'm experiencing this with her is the best high I'll ever get.

I pull over to the curb, and she gets in before I have the chance to jump out and open the door for her.

She shyly tucks a strand of hair behind her ear. "Hey."

"Hey, babe." I cup her cheeks between my hands and brush my lips against hers. "You ready to do this?"

She eagerly nods and buckles her seat belt. "I am *so* ready."

---

THE DOCTOR'S office is on the second floor of a small medical building.

Elevator music plays in the waiting room while Grace and I sit side by side. My knee is bouncing up and down to the beat while we wait for her name to be called. Two other couples and a woman are in the waiting room. One couple is going back and forth about baby names, the other a grocery list, while the woman is on her phone. No one is paying attention to us, but in the back of my mind, I wonder if they think I'm the father of Grace's baby.

With a light laugh, she rests her hand on my thigh, calming it. "I think you're more nervous than I am."

I swallow. "I think you might be right."

She starts to reply, but a nurse interrupts, "Grace Mitchell."

We stand, and I ball up my fist, stopping myself from grabbing Grace's hand. This isn't something normal for us, and I'm not sure what to do. We've held hands aplenty, but for some reason, this moment feels different.

I stand to the side as the nurse takes Grace's weight and

blood pressure before leading us into a room. Grace sits on the exam table while answering the nurse's questions. As soon as the nurse leaves, I scoot my chair as close to Grace as possible. Before we can make conversation, my gaze whips to the door at the sound of a knock.

"Come in," Grace calls out.

The ultrasound tech walks in with an eager smile. "Hi, guys! My name is Sylvia, and I'll be doing your ultrasound. Today's the day we'll learn the sex of the baby. Is that something you'd like to know?"

Grace tucks a curl of hair behind her ear. "I'm so ready for it."

Grace's attitude toward being pregnant is changing. At first, it was shock and almost dread of keeping the secret and feeling alone. As time has passed, she's been growing more comfortable with the idea of becoming a mother. Some days, she pulls up her shirt to show off how fast her belly is growing. She recites excerpts of the baby books she's been reading. It's no longer fear. It's excitement. Sure, I see the nervousness in her eyes at times, but that never beats out how breathtaking it is to watch her face light up while she talks about having a baby.

As far as the sex, she hasn't told me what she wants. Our friends have asked a few times, but she always tells them it doesn't matter to her. No matter what, I know the baby will be loved by Grace like no other.

The redheaded tech's attention turns to me.

"This is Finn," Grace bursts out as if feeling the need to define who I am.

She pauses, her mouth opening, and I can see the wheels turning in her head as to what to introduce me as.

I straighten in my chair. "I'm the father."

# CHAPTER TWENTY-SIX

# Grace

"IT'S A GIRL!" Finn shouts again when we get into his car. He grabs my face and kisses me. "We're having a girl!"

It's been an emotional day.

Before leaving the school, Gavin questioned where I was going.

To which I told him none of his damn business.

Finn then introduced himself as the father of my baby.

I nearly collapsed when he did, but it created a moment of relief.

And we found out the sex.

"A girl," I squeal against his lips.

As the last word leaves my mouth, I feel his smile drop against it. He pulls away and grimaces as if he'd been slapped in the face.

With wide eyes, he says, "I mean ... you're having a girl." All excitement in his tone has vanished.

Each word said with sadness.

His face is unreadable.

But I know what he's thinking.

Why he corrected himself.

*We're* not having a girl. I am.

This isn't his baby.

As fun as it's been to pretend, reality is here.

Her father is a man I despise—one inferior to the one next to me.

Her father isn't the one who nearly jumped out of his seat in excitement when the tech delivered the good news. It tears me up that I did this to my baby. I should've been smarter about who I slept with, but in the end, I'll never regret having her.

Is the timing wrong? Yes.

Is it with the wrong person? Yes.

*But how can I regret something I already love so much?*

I could ask Finn to step up, but it's unfair to put that weight on him. We've only been dating a short time, and this is the first serious relationship he's ever been in. Everything is great now, but throw in the responsibilities of a newborn later, and he might realize it's not what he wants.

Finn clears his throat and shakes his head as he braces his hands against the steering wheel. "Sorry, I guess I got in a little over my head." He squeezes his eyes shut. "I don't know what that little girl will be to me, Grace."

I hunch my shoulders forward and sit in silence.

"I just don't want to get attached." He withdraws his hands from the steering wheel, and they fall limp in his lap.

I swallow, struggling for words.

This is a Finn I've never seen before—a broken, confused man.

All because of me.

I caused this.

My ribs suddenly feel too tight as my heart hammers against it.

"I don't want to get too attached," Finn says, staring ahead. "And then lose everything."

Tears pool in my eyes. "I'm sorry I put you in this position." I shrink into my seat. "It was unfair and selfish of me to do so. I'm truly sorry. If I could take it back, I would."

He whips his attention to me, his face twisting in betrayal. "Take back our relationship? The time we've spent together?" He gestures between us. "I'm confused and hurt that you said you'd take *back* what the hell we've created here." His lower lip trembles. "I'm already confused because I'm falling so hard for you, growing so attached to not only you but also to the little one who'll soon be in this world."

I stare at him with intent. "What ... what are you saying?"

"I'm saying that I want to be just as much in her world as yours." His statement is said with complete certainty.

"You say that now, but what about when she's born?" My chest hitches. "It'll be different ... overwhelming. It's a lot to ask of someone. What if you wake up in the morning and decide you no longer want that responsibility?"

"That won't happen," he rushes out.

"Your life can change. You could meet someone else—"

He stills. "Meet someone? Like another woman?"

I nod, sniffling back tears as my chin trembles.

"Fuck that," he enunciates each word. "I don't want *another woman*. Have you seen me open up myself with another woman like I have with you? Hell, I moved in with you." He smacks his hands together with each point he makes. "I'm here for you through your pregnancy because it's *you*. I don't want another woman. My feelings, my *love*, for you and the baby will never change."

"Finn," I sigh, taking his hand, "I'm just scared. I don't want to lose you."

And after years of hiding behind our feelings, our friendship, Finn and I are finally letting everything come to light. No longer can we hold anything in because it might lead us to losing each other.

He squeezes my hand before cupping the back of my head and pulling me into him. "I'm all in, Grace. I want everything with you—marriage, kids, all of it. There will never be anyone else but you."

# CHAPTER TWENTY-SEVEN

# Finn

"YOU READY TO MEET THE PARENTS?" Brian asks while I'm on break.

I blow out an upward breath. "I wouldn't say that."

He chuckles. "Trust me, they sound more intimidating than what they are. Sure, they're strict, but once you get to know them, they're cool."

"Maybe for you." I gulp. "You fit in with them."

Brian raises a brow. "What do you mean?"

"You have a good job." I count the reasons on my fingers. "Come from money. College-educated." I thrust my thumb into my chest. "Me? I threw people out of bars and come from the slums."

He flaps his hand, dismissing my words. "You're not just a guy who threw drunk people out of bars. You're more than that, man. You're a good dude. That matters more than anything. Don't sell yourself short, Finn. I didn't think you were like that."

*Good point.*

I've never been self-deprecating.

But with Grace, it's always been the issue.

She's so damn perfect.

There will never be a day I won't question if I deserve her.

"If all else fails, I'll text you a list of her mom's favorite wines," Brian adds. "Her dad likes golf."

I throw my head back. "Good thing I don't know shit about golf."

"Google it." He flicks his finger toward the computer in front of him. "But don't mention my man, Tiger Woods."

"Why?"

"Her mom hates him after the whole cheating scandal."

"Wine, golf, but not Tiger." I snap my fingers. "Got it. Any other pointers?"

"Just stay calm and keep it cool."

"Easier said than done."

---

IF THERE'S anything that can cheer me up, it's coming home to Grace.

When I walk into the living room, she's lounging on the couch with her pregnancy pillow. Her hair is wrapped into a high ponytail, her face makeup-free, and she's wearing her fluffy purple robe.

"Hey there," she says, shooting me a flirtatious smile.

I return the smile while moving deeper into the room and toss my keys on the coffee table. "How was your day?"

*This.*

It feels so domesticated.

Like something you'd see on a damn Disney sitcom.

"Good." She yawns. "Except my feet are killing me. I thought about cutting them off a few times while the kids were at recess."

"How about I make you dinner?" I wink. "And give my babe a little foot massage."

She throws her arms back. "A foot massage. A vagina massage. I'll take all the massages."

Grace and I haven't progressed more in the hookup department. I finger her and eat her out. She jacks me off and sucks my cock. My dick hasn't been inside her yet, but I want to wait until she's ready.

Honestly, until *we're* ready.

Once we pass that mark, it'll break me if I lose her.

Knowing what it's like, being inside her, and then her leaving would kill me.

I make grilled chicken and veggies, massage every inch of her, and then she falls asleep in my arms.

---

"YOU READY FOR TOMORROW?" Grace asks.

We're in bed, a show playing in the background, but neither of us is watching. Our minds are focused on tomorrow.

I blow out a deep breath, sinking my head deeper into my pillow. "As ready as I'll ever be."

Too bad I haven't had practice for this. My dumbass never deemed it necessary in the thirty years of my life to prepare myself for meeting the parents. Eventually, I should've known the day would come when I met someone I wanted to get serious with.

From what I've learned about her parents, they're strict but not assholes. They helped with Georgia while Cohen was busting his ass to provide for her and never judged them. They also raised Grace, who is the kindest damn soul I know.

I bet if they had to choose the perfect boyfriend for Grace in a lineup, it damn sure wouldn't be me, though.

*Here I go with the self-pity bullshit.*

I'm glad we're finally getting this over with.

Not only do I have the stress of meeting the parents, but

Grace is also going to tell them she's pregnant. I have to then lie and say I'm the father. A point against me becoming their favorite person by knocking their daughter up out of wedlock. I'm already starting off on the wrong foot, and I need to work harder to make a good first impression.

Grace turns to her side, propping her chin on my bare chest while peering up at me. "They're going to love you, Finn."

I tilt my head back. "Let us pray."

She chuckles, slapping my stomach. "You know, we've never talked about your family before. What are they like?"

My stomach knots at the dreaded family question.

Yet another reason why I avoid meeting the parents.

They might ask about my family, and my life goal is to avoid that topic as much as possible.

I keep my head back, unable to look at her. "There's nothing to talk about."

She drums her fingers along my stomach. "Finn, all I know about your childhood is you're an only child. That's it. I know nothing about your parents."

Sweat builds along my hairline.

I could easily lie. I've done it before. Make up some happy story about some single dad and happily ever after bullshit. But this is Grace, and I refuse to lie to her. That's why instead of lying, I've always dodged the conversation.

No more of that.

No more hiding.

Grace knows me better than anyone and would never judge me for something I couldn't control. She'll never look down on me for my father's ways.

I stare at the ceiling and reach down to run my hand through her hair. "My mom died when I was four."

"I'm so sorry, Finn," she says, her voice soothing. "How did she die?"

"Drug overdose." My answer comes out strangled. "I don't remember much about her."

Sometimes, I hate myself for not remembering anything. The only recollection I have of my mother is from pictures my dad had before getting drunk one night and burning them.

"And your dad?" There's no change in her tone.

The moment of truth.

For the both of us.

What I'm about to say is something I've never said out loud.

My muscles tighten, causing my jaw to hurt. "I'm waiting for the day I get the call that he's dead from an overdose."

I choke back the emotions from my admission as it sends a wave of nausea through me.

The bed shifts as Grace scoots up and grips my chin, moving it slightly so we're eye to eye.

She caresses my jaw. "Wow, I had no idea. I feel bad that I haven't been there for you to talk about it with."

I shake my head. "It's not exactly something to brag about, so I keep it to myself."

She lowers her hand, capturing mine in it, and laces our fingers. "Thank you for telling me that. I love learning more about you, and whenever you're ready to open up about anything else, I'm here."

And that's why I knew it was safe for me to tell Grace this.

Other people might push for more—for every damn detail—but Grace waits, allowing me to do it on my time.

I raise a brow. "That doesn't scare you away?"

She shakes her head. "Of course not." She squeezes my hand. "Finn, you can't control the family you were born into. All you can control is the direction you've taken your life from there. You? You're not an addict, you don't make reckless decisions, and you are a good man, a hard worker, and an amazing boyfriend."

*Boyfriend.*

Heat radiates into my chest at that one word.

That one word switches up my mood, evaporating the dread of talking about my family into something better.

No matter what happens, it feels damn good to say that Grace Mitchell is my motherfucking girlfriend, and I'm never letting her go. No, if I can have it my way, Grace Mitchell will be my motherfucking wife.

# CHAPTER TWENTY-EIGHT

# Grace

SCREW the people who said you get used to morning sickness.

I hope you get splinters in your feet.

If there was anything in this world I could damn to hell, it'd be morning sickness.

Scooting away from the toilet, I slouch against the wall and wipe my mouth.

"Again?" Finn asks, walking into the bathroom.

"Again." I swipe away sweat from my cheek.

He kneels down in front of me, bare-chested and wearing only gym shorts. "If I could, I'd trade places with you in a heartbeat."

He leans in to kiss me, but I swat him away.

"Vomit breath," I say, cringing.

He chuckles before planting a kiss on my forehead. "I'd still kiss you, vomit breath and all."

"I sincerely suggest you see a professional for making that comment."

He stands. "You want me to make you breakfast?"

I raise a brow. "A baby-friendly vodka smoothie?" A grin

spreads across my vomit lips. "I'll let you add kale to make it fun and healthy."

"Eggs and bacon, coming right up."

I grab the towel I was using to wipe my forehead and throw it at him as he starts to leave the room. "That isn't the support the baby books suggest!"

I'm sure the baby isn't the only one to blame for the nausea.

My nerves are on overdrive about telling my parents today.

On top of that, I'll be lying to them about who Finn is.

Well, halfway lying.

I'll tell them I love him—truth.

That we're dating—another truth.

That I plan to be with him as long as I can—fact.

That he's the one who knocked me up—big, fat lie.

I shouldn't be as worried as I am. It's not like my parents will disown me.

They'll just be *disappointed*.

Disappointment is worse than anything.

It's them saying they had better expectations for me.

He turns to look at me, bracing the doorframe with his hand. "It won't be that bad, babe. I'll be by your side all day."

THIS HAS BEEN the longest I've gone without seeing my parents.

Not even when I was in college was it this long.

I probably would've tried for longer had my mother not left a voicemail, threatening to show up at my house and work if I didn't attend family dinner today. I'm surprised it took her this long. I went from seeing them every week to being a no-show for months. They have to know something is up. The question is, what do they think it is?

Wiping my sweaty hand down my dress, I cast a curious

glance at Finn when he drives up the long driveway to my
parents' house.

"Wow," Finn comments, staring at the two-story white-
bricked home. "This is a nice place." His gaze casts to me. "Have
you lived here your entire life?"

I shake my head. "We moved here in my teens, and I moved
out after college."

My mind wanders to where we lived before and how I
preferred it. The fireplace was warmer. The living room cozier.
The pantry and my bedroom larger. I wanted to live there
forever, but then it became tainted—nothing but a reminder of
what'd happened there. So, we ran away to this home, hoping
it'd become our new favorite.

"You ready for this?"

Finn tenderly brushing my arm drags me out of my
thoughts.

"I am," I lie, unbuckling my seat belt and gripping the door
handle.

Finn is already nervous. Me telling him how anxious I am
would only make it worse for him. We get out of the car, and he
meets me at my door, taking my hand in his. With every step we
take up the walkway, I second-guess myself. When we reach my
mother's flower bed, scattered with roses and tulips, I halt,
taking a moment to prepare myself.

At least it's only pretending about one thing.

Not a relationship.

The sweet scent of my mother's favorite cherry candle
welcomes us. As if they knew we were here, my parents are
waiting for us in the foyer. Dropping Finn's hand, I curl my
arms around my stomach to hide it. I chose a loose-fitting dress
for today, but that doesn't mean I'm not apprehensive about my
growing belly. I'm not showing *that* much, but there's a baby
bump you can't miss if you pay close attention.

My mother, her hair color the same as mine but shorter,

stands in front of us, wearing an emerald dress with gemstone earrings. Her gaze is scrutinizing as if her brain is working to find out why I've been dodging them. I fail to meet her eyes and swiftly move them to my father. He's a tall man, on the skinny side, and his face is unreadable—as per usual.

He's not looking at me. No, his gaze is focused on Finn—full of concern and caution.

I chew on my lower lip, wishing I'd mentioned Finn would be with me. I'd stupidly left out I was bringing a plus-one.

Needing to take the lead on this one, I exhale a deep breath. "Mom. Dad." I drop one of my hands to motion to Finn. "This is Finn. My ... boyfriend. Finn, these are my parents, Tyra and Gregory."

It's Finn's turn to be scrutinized by my mother. She's assessing him as she does her clients. Finn dressed for the occasion—a black button-up shirt, dark jeans—and his hair is freshly cut.

I clear my throat, dragging my mom back into the conversation.

She shoots Finn a polite smile. "It's nice to meet you, Finn." Her eyes briefly move to my stomach, as if she knows, but everyone turns to the door when it swings open.

The sun beams through the doorway as Raven sprints into the house, one of her sandals flying off in the process.

"Grandma! Grandpa! We're here!" she shouts, nearly tripping as she hugs my father's legs. "And we brought cherry cobbler! Mommy lied and told Daddy she made it, but we really picked it up from the bakery."

I cover my mouth to mask my snort.

Finn chuckles.

"Hey!" Faith says as she and Brian join us. "We need to work on your snitching, kid."

I squeeze my belly, grateful for their appearance, saving me from the possible awkward moment of my mother asking questions I don't want to answer. I have yet to decide how I'll break the news. Finn asked me on the drive here, but I told him I was still working on it.

"It might be best for you to fill me in, though," Finn commented.

"I'll send you a text," I told him.

"What?" he stuttered. "We're going to discuss the plan via text in front of them?"

We went back and forth until he agreed to just wing it.

Last night, I'd thought I had the perfect plan—tell them right before leaving and then make a dash to my car. It would stop a face-to-face conversation. Everyone knows there isn't a more stressful conversation than one in person.

Give me a phone call.

A text.

Easy-peasy.

Looking someone in the eyes while speaking about something sensitive?

Hard stuff.

To master that plan, I first have to sit through dinner and manage to keep my mouth shut.

---

"NO WINE?"

I nearly drop my glass at my mother's question.

We just sat down for dinner, and I declined my mother's offer for a glass of wine. Her eyes widened when I said I was sticking with water for tonight. Like with my friends, that's a sure sign something is off. My mom would've definitely expected at least a glass from me, given I just brought a new man home.

Everyone's eyes are on me.

This is the moment I realize I suck at secrets.

"I'm pregnant."

All I hear is my mother's glass shattering to the tiles.

# CHAPTER TWENTY-NINE

# Finn

I TOLD Grace it was a mistake not to have a Telling Them You're Pregnant plan, but she said she wouldn't know until the time came. Us deciding on a strategy would've stopped the slight armpit rings hidden by the dark color of my shirt and would've stopped the ache in my throat that's been there since we got into my car.

Knowing Grace, I was certain she couldn't hold in the news all night until we left.

I at least thought she'd make it past dinner.

My heart gallops in my chest. It's been doing that since the moment I walked into the Mitchells' home.

Not only because I was meeting them for the first time.

Scratch that. I was only meeting *her mom* for the first time.

I was certain her dad recognized me—just what I'd been afraid of.

I've fucked up in my life, but every mistake I've made, I learned from.

I've changed.

But no matter what, I'm my father's son.

And that motherfucking sucks.

Brian scoots out his chair and grabs the glass from the floor.

"It's fine," Tyra rushes out, stopping him. "Just leave it."

Her voice is shaky. Her face pales.

Everyone, even Raven, is quiet, waiting on her parents' reaction.

Brian ignores her request, snags the shattered pieces, and places them on the table. He pours her another glass. Tyra grabs it, chugs down the wine, and pours herself another.

Moving my attention from her, I focus on Gregory.

He clears his throat. "I take it, you're the father?" Like before, his face is unreadable.

*Does anyone ever know what this man is thinking?*

*No.*

That's probably why he's so good at his job.

"I sure hope so," Tyra cries out, gaping at me.

Grace pays me a quick glance and nods. "He is."

I wonder how well they know their daughter.

There's more than nervousness in Grace's tone.

She's not a good liar, and had I not known the situation, I'd have known she was lying.

I lower my hand under the table and capture hers, giving it a squeeze of assurance that I have her back, no matter what.

*We've got this.*

"I am," I repeat, my voice clear and controlled.

Tyra's gaze whips to Faith. "Did you know your sister was pregnant?"

"Yes," Faith says with a shrug. "I think it's amazing." She motions toward me with her wineglass. "Finn is a good guy, and I think they'll make great parents."

I am a big Faith fan.

She and Brian are good people.

Tyra gasps. Obviously, she has a flair for the dramatic.

She stares at Faith, stunned. "You knew and didn't tell us?"

Faith lifts the glass to her lips and says into it, "Not my news to tell."

"Does that mean Aunt Grace has a baby in her belly?" Raven asks, chomping on a dinner roll.

"It sure does," Faith replies.

Raven jumps out of her seat. "Can I see?"

Faith catches her arm before Raven passes her. "I don't think so. Aunt Grace will show you her belly another time."

Raven pouts while returning to her seat. "You promise, Aunt Grace?"

Grace's lower lip trembles as she nods. "Yes."

The herb-roasted chicken gets neglected as a result of the news.

The questions start.

All coming from Tyra and none from Gregory.

He throws in comments, but no drilling comes from him.

I wish I could climb into his brain and figure out what the fuck he's thinking.

We tell them we started dating a few months ago.

The pregnancy wasn't planned.

I plan on being there for her.

Tyra questions if we're getting married, but luckily, Faith asks a question to detour us away from that conversation. When Tyra tries to go back to the subject, Grace tells her we're focused on the baby at the moment. I gulp, wanting to tell them that I'd marry Grace tomorrow if she'd have me. But Grace is taking the lead, and I'm only speaking when absolutely necessary.

We explain how we've been friends for years.

By the time dinner is over, I'm exhausted.

Tyra seems more comfortable now that she's better informed. In fact, she seems excited about having another grandchild.

Tyra asks Grace and Faith to help her in the kitchen, and I

use that moment to go to the bathroom. I'm in need of a moment alone before my head explodes. On my way back to the dining room, I admire the home, passing expensive artwork, a curved staircase, and a billiard room.

"Finn."

I turn suddenly at the sound of my name to find Gregory standing inches from me. He shoves his hands into the pockets of his black slacks, and unease lines his features as we stare each other down.

His staredown isn't one of intimidation.

It's more along the lines of wanting to know what the fuck I'm planning to do with his daughter.

"Let's talk." A harsh sigh leaves him before he jerks his head toward an open door.

I nod. "All right."

Shit is about to get awkward real quick.

I follow him into an office filled with dark bookshelves lined with law books. He circles the massive desk, rolls out an executive chair, and sits—his posture near perfect. Clasping his hands together, he rests them onto the desk.

"Have a seat," he demands.

I ease into the chair, doing my best to match his posture and not slouch. I wait for his interrogation ... or threats to stay the fuck away from his daughter. Although the chance of him scaring me away from her will be harder in his eyes because he's under the impression his daughter is having a baby with me.

"Does Grace know about your past?" he sternly asks.

That's the question I've been terrified of.

The reason I took so long to take my relationship further with Grace.

I didn't want her to know about my past.

I told her about my family, but what her father knows? It's deeper.

It's humiliating.

But she does deserve to know.

"She doesn't," I reply, hating the hint of shame in my voice from keeping this from her. It's embarrassing that I haven't been as open and honest with her as I should've been.

"I figured so." He expels a long breath, and his eyes are serious when they level on me. "Finn, I'm well aware that people make mistakes. Every day, I look at people's mistakes and decide the consequences of them. Their future is in my hands. For as long as I've been a judge, I pride myself on reading people well. I'm pro second chance because people learn, and as bad as it seems, some are given shitty cards in their game of life. When they're young, it can take a minute to figure out the best way to play them. Along the journey, they might break the law." He hesitates and holds up a finger. "Sometimes, good people break the law because they don't want to starve or for their families to go without." His voice turns low and even. "The day you walked into my courtroom, I knew it was because of the cards you'd been handed. You weren't some punk kid breaking the law for fun. You were a *survivor*. The second time, I'll admit, I wasn't happy about it, but there was something in my gut that told me to give you another chance—that you weren't some hardened criminal who'd do wrong in society. You had a bad family—no offense—and you needed to escape their ways."

My brain flashes back to those times I saw him in the courtroom. I was fourteen and fifteen, scared out of my motherfucking mind over what would happen. I didn't want to go to juvie, but I also needed food. My pride wouldn't let me ask others for help—not to eat, not for school supplies, not for basic necessities. So, I shoplifted the shit I needed because I saw that as a better option in my immature eyes. I stopped the petty crimes after Judge Mitchell—aka Gregory, aka Grace's father—told me that was my last chance.

"I know your family," he continues. "I was aware of the household you were growing up in. And frankly, I was relieved you were only shoplifting, not robbing homes, doing drugs, or harming others." He shakes his head and scoffs, "You were barely a teen, stealing food, cough medicine, and ibuprofen."

I shut my eyes at the memory. I was so sick. I called my dad for hours, only for him to tell me to stick a cold washcloth on my forehead and take some ibuprofen. When I told him we didn't have any, he told me *tough shit* and to sleep off my fever. I was miserable, so I shoved on my boots and walked a half-mile to the local convenience store, not giving a shit about being busted because even if I got arrested, the jail had to have some damn medicine.

Gregory taps his desk, a wrinkle creasing along his forehead in concentration. "After that final warning, I never saw you in my courtroom again. I did, however, see you bagging groceries at the market six months later. It made me proud that I'd seen you were a good kid and not thrown you to the wolves." He smiles for the first time tonight; it's a timid one, as he's still wary of my role in his daughter's life. "My Grace, she's understanding." He snorts. "Way more understanding than most. Be honest with her. She deserves to know the past of the man she's having a child with."

I do the first thing that comes to mind.

I salute him. "Yes, sir."

And then I feel like a fucking idiot for doing so.

*Do people in their circle salute each other?*

His smile widens, not making me feel so much like a dumbass.

Then, his lips press into a thin line. "And don't break her heart."

I lift my head high and wait until his eyes meet mine before answering, "I won't."

If there's any certainty I have in life, it's that.

I'll never hurt Grace Mitchell.

"If it's worth anything, I think you'll be an amazing father."

That statement.

It's as if he'd just told me I won the lottery.

That I'd have happiness for the rest of my life.

*"You'll be an amazing father."*

It's everything I've ever wanted to hear because it's everything I've always been terrified of. I don't have a good dad. Neither did my dad. Bad dads run in my DNA, and I've always worried about whether I'd break that curse.

I gratefully bow my head. "Thank you."

He gives me a strong, decisive nod before standing. "I'm here if you need anything. Brian has seemed to already taken a liking to you. Anything Grace, the baby, or *you* need, don't hesitate to come to us. My biggest priority has always been my family, and it seems you've now joined it."

Nearly speechless, I repeat, "Thank you."

He stares at me in expectation. "On another note, do you plan to marry her?"

# CHAPTER THIRTY

# Grace

"TONIGHT DIDN'T GO AS bad as I'd expected," I tell Finn when we get home.

But it also didn't go as well as I'd hoped.

My mother's reaction was dramatic, to say the least.

Which is weird because she tends to be the most level-headed person I know. I guess not seeing your daughter in months and then learning she was randomly knocked up might lead a parent to that sort of reaction.

He nods. "It didn't."

"You want to tell me what my father said in his office?"

After I was done helping my mom in the kitchen, Finn was nowhere to be found. When I asked Brian where he was, he said my father had stopped him on his way back from the bathroom and that they were in his office. My father is a fair man, but he's also not one to beat around the bush. He speaks his mind and reads people well, considering that's his job. Whatever they talked about in that office, I hope to God it doesn't scare Finn away.

It's not like Finn is required to stay if it does.

It's times like this that I remember he's not the father and he isn't obligated to be here.

Finn's back straightens before he releases a deep breath and sits on the couch. "We need to talk." He pats the space next to him with a fixed look of concentration on his face.

*Oh God.*

*Here it comes.*

There wasn't much conversation on the ride home. We laughed about Raven's request to see my belly, not reading the room whatsoever.

The nervousness I had earlier returns with a vengeance.

I take slow steps to the couch and carefully sit down. Out of recent habit, my hand rests against my stomach. Finn gently smiles when he notices my movement before placing his hand over mine. We sit like this for a moment—our hands over the reason our relationship has changed, the reason our lives will change.

Finn clears his throat. "Today isn't the first time I've met your father."

I grow quiet, chewing the inside of my cheek before saying, "Okay?"

*Where is he going with this?*

*Does he mean they met at the grocery store?*

*Did my dad find out we were hanging out and confront him?*

Finn rubs his eyebrow. "I got into some trouble, and your dad was my judge."

"Oh ..." My voice wavers with just that one word. "And what kind of trouble did you get into?"

His hand doesn't leave my belly. "When I was a minor, I did stupid shit. Shit I'm not proud of."

"Can you define *shit you're not proud of*?"

*What does one define as stupid shit when breaking the law?*

*Punching someone?*

*Stealing?*

*Or killing?*

"Shoplifting. Petty theft. I stole things I needed to survive because no one else had provided them for me."

My shoulders relax at his answer.

I know Finn hasn't had it easy. Not only from the admission about his parents last night. He's made random comments about his life. Unlike some of our friends, he doesn't talk about his parents. But also, like others, like Cohen and Georgia, he seems to agree with them when conversations of having terrible parents come up. I've heard stories of Finn coming from nothing and rising above it. And if my father had been worried Finn would be a threat to me, he'd have kicked his ass out of his house.

"Finn," I whisper, stopping until I have all this attention. "I'd never judge you for that. You had a crappy childhood and had to do things you're not proud of." My mouth turns dry at my next question. "Did he give you jail time?"

"Nah." Finn shakes his head. "He let me off the hook both times."

I smile. "That means he thought you were a good kid."

"I guess so." He pulls his hand away and turns on the cushion to face me. "Are you sure you want your baby around someone like that? Who's been in trouble with the law?"

I hold back from telling him his question is stupid.

Maybe it's dumb to me, but from the distraught look in Finn's eyes, it's something that scares him. Losing me—losing *us*—terrifies the man sitting next to me with tears nearly in his eyes.

I speak softly, "Finn, I wouldn't want any other man to be with us."

## CHAPTER THIRTY-ONE

# Finn

I FALL down on the couch and replay Grace's words through my head.

I grin.

Reveling in them.

Pushing them so deep into my brain in hopes that they'll stay there forever.

I sweep my gaze to her. Affection glows in them.

*I want this woman.*

Physically—because damn, my dick gets hard when I just look at her. *And* it is hard.

But not just in that way.

I want her emotionally.

And I want her *forever*.

"Grace," I say her name like a demand.

I'm not sure who goes for it first, but one moment, we're side by side on the couch, and the next, our lips are connected. Our kiss is intense and intimate. Shifting, I grip her hips, positioning her on her back, and crawl over her. The couch is small, and there isn't much room, but that won't stop me from touching my girl. I have one foot on the floor, and my other knee is pushed into the couch cushion. We don't break our kiss, and I groan when Grace rotates her hips, pushing her core up against me. Thrusting my tongue into her mouth, I claim her as we dry-hump on the couch.

My heart races as I push up her dress, lift my hand, and play with the string of her panties with one finger.

"Baby," I whisper against her lips, "you're soaked."

Her panties are the wettest they've ever been. Her pussy is ready for me.

My heart races. We've messed around some, but never have we had anything this emotionally charged. I've touched her, tasted her, but we haven't crossed any lines beyond that. Tonight, shit's changed. We're baring our all to each other, sharing a connection deeper than friendship and hooking up. We've said the *I love you*, but now, we're exposing our true selves. The deeper we fall into each other, the deeper that love grows.

All the issues I had been worried would push Grace away did the opposite. I told her my past, and she only wanted me more. I've made it clear I want her to be my future. Her parents accepted her pregnancy *and me*. There's nothing that can hold us back any longer. It's as if we were waiting for the pieces to come together before passing the final line of intimacy.

Pulling back, I gently caress her jaw. "I love you, Grace. I love you more than I've ever loved anyone in my life." No one will ever mean as much to me as she does. "It's always been you."

Her eyes widen, and we stare at each other, nearly in a trance.

Her breathing quickens, and when I peek down, her chest is heaving in and out.

Reaching out, she runs her hand over my neck before gripping the back of it. "Then make love to me."

"Are you going to give me all of you?" I bury my face in the curve of her neck. "Are you mine?"

"Yes," she whispers, shivering as I suck on her neck. "Always."

*Yes.*

*Always.*

I fall back, sliding off her, and bring myself to my feet. Holding out my hand, I help her up. As much as I'd like to make this sexier—throw her over my shoulder or some shit like that—I don't want to hurt her. I lead her to the bedroom, and as soon as I turn on the lights, my lips return to hers. I walk her to the bed and tenderly lay her down on her back.

Desire rushes through me, and I'd love to make this quick. To pull off her panties and shove inside her, giving it to her hard and rough. But that's not how I want my first time with Grace to be. It needs to be special, memorable, and better for her than for me.

Grace stares at me, licking her lips, as I unbutton my shirt and toss it over my shoulder. The chill of the room smacks into my back as I lower myself over her. My dick twitches under my pants the moment it makes the slightest brush against Grace's body.

*Dear God, don't let me nut this early. Please.*

I moan when she urgently attempts to bend forward, but it's not easy for her.

Frustrated, she falls back and frowns. "Take off your pants *right now*. I would, but this prego body doesn't make it easy for me to rip off your clothes."

I chuckle. "I guess I can do the job for you." With a smirk, I waste no time in giving in to her demand. Popping my zipper open, I slightly climb off her in order to kick them, along with my boxer briefs, off. My cock springs forward, aching for her, and she gasps.

I stroke it. "Is this what you want?"

I never thought I'd be talking to Grace like this or jerking myself off as Grace wriggles underneath me, licking her lips. Her eyes are glued to my hand moving up and down my cock, as if it's the best thing she's ever watched.

"You want me to fuck you with this?"

She nods, and it shocks the shit out of me when she says, "If you don't *right now*, then I'm going to stick my own fingers in my panties and get myself off."

"We can't have that, can we?" I wink, dropping my hand from my cock and moving back up her body. Planting a soft kiss to her lips, I flick down the straps of her dress, lowering them, and drag it down her body before tossing it the same way I did with my clothes.

My mouth waters at the sight of her wearing only a bra and panties. Dropping my head between her thighs, I suck her clit over her panties. She arches her back, gasping, and unsnaps her bra at the same time. Giving her one final flick of my tongue, I peel her panties down her legs. I fall back to take a good look at the woman I love.

Her breathing is deep. Her breasts bounce with every movement of the chest. Her belly moves the same way.

Before thinking, I kiss her stomach, rubbing my hand over it, and say, "You are so fucking gorgeous."

Her eyes shut, and her shoulders relax.

Lowering my hand, I run a finger through her wet slit. "I can't wait to fuck you, baby. It's going to feel so good."

She squirms underneath me. "Then get to it. *Fuck me*, Finn."

And with those dirty words that rarely leave Grace's mouth, I make one hard thrust inside her. She releases a loud moan, her back moving higher than it was when I sucked on her clit. Bracing myself, I collapse my body over hers, holding myself up with a hand on each side of her head. I still inside her and tell myself to slow down. I change positions, rotating my hips from side to side, hoping to hit every sensitive spot inside her. Her nails dig into my arms, deeper and deeper every time I rock inside her. Her pussy is so tight, so wet, and so fucking amazing.

My cock has never been in a pussy this wet and tight.

Then I freeze.

*Fuck!*

She stops, staring at me in confusion.

"I'm not wearing a condom," I breathe out.

I've never barebacked anyone before. It's not that she can get pregnant, but I don't know what she's comfortable with.

She points at her belly. "Not like I can get knocked up again."

"I'm clean," I confirm. "Never had sex without a condom ... and it's been a while."

"Same," she whispers. "I got tested as soon as I found out about Gavin."

With those words, I return to making love to her.

Slowly sliding in and out of the woman I love.

She tilts her hips up, meeting me thrust for thrust until it's no longer slow and sensual.

It's fast, hungry, and raw.

"Swear to God, Grace"—I peer down at her, sweat building along my forehead—"after this, I will give it to you so slow."

She smiles. "Good, but now, I want it harder." She pushes her waist up, circling her hips so her clit rubs against my groin, and moans. "Get me off. *Please.*"

Our moans, our heavy breathing, fill the room.

It's a struggle, but I wait until she's gasping my name below me, until her knees buckle up and she gets off, before I come inside her.

# CHAPTER THIRTY-TWO

# Grace

I FALL BACK against the sheets in exhaustion.

It's been a weekend of sex.

Missionary.

Doggy.

Me on top—my first time thirty minutes ago.

In our bed.

On the couch.

In the shower—which was difficult for a pregnant woman, but Finn seemed to situate us perfectly. It's a plus, having a strong man. Gavin's skinny ass would've never been able to hold me up while also thrusting inside me.

Unlike getting rid of morning sickness, the rumors about horniness when you're pregnant are true. I've never wanted sex —never wanted intimacy—as much as I do with Finn. I've never experienced a happiness like this before, and I've never felt safer in his arms.

And now, we finished morning sex.

*Early as heck in the morning* sex.

Finn woke me up with his head between my legs, and then we ended our romp with his cock between them.

"I think this is the only time I'll like mornings," Finn says, catching his breath.

"Glad I could change that for you." I yawn and groan at the same time. "And you're keeping me up quite late and changing that for me."

"That's because you're irresistible, babe."

---

I'VE NEVER CONSIDERED STABBING anyone.

Until now.

"Good morning," Gavin says with a mischievous smirk as he walks into my classroom.

I cast a glance at the scissors chilling in my pen holder.

*Could I say it was an accident?*

I could stab him somewhere that'd leave no permanent damage, like his foot or something. His foot would be nice because then the jackass couldn't stroll into my classroom, looking like the smug jerk he is. All I know is his presence here will ruin my happiness of what this weekend gave me. I can't let that happen.

Ignoring him and the stabby urge, I grab my phone and pretend to text.

"Oh, come on." He inches farther into my classroom. "Can't you show a little more excitement to see me?"

"I'm not excited to see you," I deadpan. "In fact, it'd make me very excited if you turned and left, and I never had to see you again. That'd make my day."

He tsks. "I remember when you liked me. Our conversations went so much better."

"Then I learned you were a cheating scumbag," I chirp.

"How's our baby?"

His question sends fire through my veins.

My phone falls from my hand and onto my desk.

He receives the reaction he wanted.

It's been weeks since he's mentioned the baby. I hoped he would find me ignoring him an easy escape from taking responsibility for what he'd done to not only me but also to his wife and children.

What would be a better outcome for hiding you'd cheated and knocked a woman up than the other woman not being able to stand the sight of you now?

"You need to get out of my room," I grind out. My gaze flicks back to the scissors.

"No can do." He arrogantly lifts his chin. "I'll be sitting in and watching you teach today. Make sure you're doing your job."

I ignore him in an attempt to get him to leave.

"Who's the guy who keeps visiting you?"

I grip the edge of my desk and push my chair out. "That's none of your business."

He gives me a spiteful smile. "As the father of your child, I think it is."

"You know what? I'll leave." I stand and do my best to storm out of the classroom, although my pace is on the slower side, given my pregnancy.

Passing the teachers' lounge, I make a right to Georgia's office and knock on the door. As much as I want to confide in Finn about Gavin's taunting, it'll lead to nothing but trouble. If Finn finds out Gavin is messing with me, he'll kick his ass.

Without waiting for an answer and hoping she isn't busy, I open the door and burst into her office. I'm out of breath—both from the baby weight and scurrying away from Gavin as fast as I could. I need to take a seat.

"Good morning, babe," Georgia says, not even affected by my sudden entry. "I have to say, the baby bump is looking hot on you, Mama."

I sink back in a chair, sitting in front of the desk she's

perched behind. I'm still getting used to seeing my free-spirited friend—former boutique and part-time bar employee—have a behind-the-desk job. She started working here—taking the place of the retired school counselor—not too long ago, and I couldn't be happier. There's nothing better than working with your best friend.

I frown down at my belly. "I feel ... unhot."

The high of my weekend has been shot down to ashes, thanks to Gavin.

"Wrong, and I'm positive Finn would state otherwise." She tosses a stack of papers away from her and tightens one of her two buns on the top of her head. "How are you two doing, by the way?"

I texted Georgia the night I told my parents about the pregnancy—post amazing sex with Finn. I told her it went well, but that was all she got before Finn was ready for round two.

Affection spreads through me at the mention of Finn. It erases a smidgen of the anger Gavin dragged out of me this morning.

"We're good," I reply. "I was scared things would change after he met my parents, but it's only gotten better." I refrain from telling her that Finn had already met my father. I'm not sure who all knows about Finn's juvenile run-ins with the law, but I won't be the one to ever tell them.

Her eyebrows squish together. "Then why do you look like they canceled Snickers bars?"

My head pounds. "Gavin paid me a visit in my classroom."

"Ugh, is the bastard still giving you a hard time?"

I reluctantly nod. "I pray he gets fired every day."

"Report him."

"And say what?" I throw up my arms in defeat. "I didn't know he was married and slept with him?"

"No. You tell them he's practically harassing you."

I swallow down my fear of having to take it that far. "He'll get bored of me. I'm just waiting it out."

"No one can get bored of you, babe, so I wouldn't count on that happening." She takes a sip of her iced coffee. "You need to stick it to the man where it hurts. Report him or ... I don't know ... tell his wife what a piece of shit he is."

She—along with Cassidy, Lola, and Sierra—have told me to tell his wife. It's the right thing to do, and I'd want my husband's mistress to come to me. Confrontation makes me nauseous, and I try to prevent it at all costs. If I went to his wife, I'd be going head-to-head with her because she'd ask questions that I'd have to answer. And who knows if she'd even believe me?

"If you don't want to tell her, I'll tell her." Georgia shrugs. "I'll mention that there are rumors that he's been having an affair with another woman. I won't even say it's someone who works here."

Georgia is always the one who comes up with the wild plans—ones that usually lead straight to trouble.

"No, that's not necessary." I run my hand over the few wrinkles in my floral dress. "I'll wait it out."

I stand at the sound of the bell, and we make plans to meet for lunch before I return to my classroom.

---

"YOU HOMEWRECKING WHORE."

I tense in my chair at the shrill voice screaming those words. At the same time I lift my head, a woman comes barreling into my classroom—her waddle-walk similar to mine.

Even though it's only the second time I've seen her, I know who she is. I'd recognize her from across the grocery store because the first time I laid eyes on her, she introduced herself as Gavin's wife to everyone in the office. That's also the day when I refrained from introducing myself as Gavin's mistress ... and the day I broke things off with him.

I jump at the sound of my classroom door slamming shut as she stares at me with murderous eyes.

Her orange maxi dress sways from side to side as she grows closer. "You've been fucking my husband behind my back."

From her appearance, you wouldn't think words like that would fall from her lips in public—that she wouldn't make a scene at her husband's place of employment. She's nearly the opposite of me. Curvy—with a breast size I would kill for. Her black hair is cut into a bob, hitting the curve of her shoulders. Briefly, I wonder what Gavin's other mistresses looked like because I'm almost certain there are/have been others.

Swallowing hard, I hold up my hands, palms facing her. "Whoa, I'm not screwing your husband."

She thrusts the phone in her hand in my direction. "That's not what the texts between you and him say. I looked through his phone!"

When I stand, she gasps at the sight of my belly. "I had no idea Gavin was married. As soon as I found out, I broke things off."

She blinks at me. "How do you not know when someone is married?"

I sigh. "It seems your husband was as good at hiding that he was married as he was at cheating on you. The man lies, and I want nothing to do with him."

"And the baby?" She gestures to my stomach. "It's his?"

I turn quiet, refusing to look at her.

"Wow." She seethes, her lips forming a thin line. "It is."

"I don't want anything from him," I rush out, my cheeks burning. "To be honest, I'd prefer if he were out of the picture."

Maybe she'll make that happen. If I caught my husband having an affair in the workplace, I wouldn't be comfortable with him keeping that job with her.

"You'd prefer him to be out of your life?" she snarks. "Real nice, considering you ruined our marriage."

"I ruined nothing," I bite out. "As I said, I had no idea he was married until the first day you came into the school."

She's not digesting my words. Her outrage overtakes any reasoning she has. Her confronting me isn't an attempt to get answers. She needs someone to take her anger out on.

"Stay away from my husband," she demands, spit flying from her mouth.

Before I tell her that's what I've been trying to do but he isn't making it easy, she charges out of the room. I release a breath of relief ... until her next show happens.

"That's right, people!" she screams in the hallway. "The woman who teaches in that room slept with my husband!"

My knees buckle, and I grip the edge of my desk to stop myself from crumpling to the floor.

*Why is she doing this to me?*

*Does she not believe I didn't know?*

If she read through Gavin's texts, she'd have seen the endless times I asked him to leave me alone.

When I confronted him for being married.

When I called him a liar.

Sick of the all-around bullshit, I push my shoulders back, lift my chin, and leave the room. My colleagues are standing in the hall, their classroom doors open, and kids' voices filter out each one of them. Humiliation rises up my cheeks, but I do a decent job of hiding it while I dodge their questions and charge toward Gavin's office. As I pass his wife, who seems to be shocked that I showed my face, I flip her off.

Georgia is standing outside his door. "You want me to kill him? I can make it look like an accident."

"No," I bite out. "That'll stop me from doing it myself."

Without knocking, I open his door and gasp. Gavin's office is destroyed—shattered picture frames on the floor, décor pieces lying next to them, a crooked painting clinging to life on the wall. The desk has been cleared of all its contents as if everything was pushed to the floor in one angry swipe.

"You got her wrath, too, it appears," Gavin says, sitting with slouched shoulders.

"Nice office," Georgia says from behind me. "I'd call this décor style *something that assholes deserve*."

I shoot Georgia a look over my shoulder. "Can you give us a moment?"

She nods. "If you need anything, I'll be outside the door ... and most definitely not listening."

"Yeah, okay," I say sarcastically, knowing her ear will most likely be against the door, listening to every single word.

I've never seen Gavin like this. He's not used to being on the other side of the provocation. He's used to being the one in control, and he's lost that. His Adam's apple bobs, and sweat has built up along his hairline. He stares at me vacantly, as if he's lost all thought process. His actions finally came back to bite him in the ass—in the worst way possible. He could lose his job for this.

"I admitted everything," Gavin says as soon as I shut the door, forcing his words through clenched teeth. "Vivica knows about us and the baby."

"So does everyone in the school," I grit out. "She announced it in the hallway."

"Fuck," he hisses, slamming his fist on the desk.

I do another scan of the room. "Did you admit it to her ... or were you caught?"

His jaw twitches. "Does it fucking matter?"

I stay quiet.

"I forgot my phone at home, and she went through it. She came here, confronted me, and I was honest with her. I should've done it before. She deserved to know I was unfaithful and no longer in love with her." His tone turns serious yet softens some. "I love *you*, Grace. I want *you*."

I glare at him. "You've lost your marbles if you think I'd ever be with you." I cross my arms and kick my foot out. "I wish I'd never met you. Now, all my coworkers know what happened." As I blink away tears, it's a struggle to keep my voice stable. "I'm taking the rest of the day off. Find someone to cover me for the mess you caused."

He reaches out toward me. "Grace—"

"I'm taking a personal day!" I shout, turning around and whipping the door open. I nearly fall into Georgia when I step out.

She flips Gavin off before turning her attention to me. "Want me to take a personal day with you? I'm totally down."

"No," I sigh. "You'd probably be his last priority to find a cover." There could be students who need her today.

"True." She hugs me while we walk out. "I'll be over as soon as I get off. And don't you worry. I'll set anyone straight who talks shit here, and I need to hunt down his crazy wife, so she'll shut the fuck up."

*Oh God.*

I forgot about her.

"Thanks, babe." I avoid Rachelle's gaze, scurrying out before she asks any questions.

As soon as I get in my car, the tears come.

I'm sobbing, my nose snotty, when I call Finn.

"What's wrong, baby?" he rushes out in panic.

I break down and tell him the situation.

"That motherfucker," he snarls. "I'm leaving work now. Do you want me to pick you up from the school?"

"No." I sniffle. "I'll meet you at home."

FINN IS WAITING for me on the porch. As soon as I pull into the driveway, he jumps down the steps and hurries to me.

"Baby," he says, wrapping his arms around me the moment I step out. "It'll be okay."

*Will it, though?*

Everyone at the school knows.

People will talk.

I could lose my job just as easily as Gavin could.

My parents will ask why.

And word will spread.

Shoot, they could know by the end of the day, given how many people they talk to.

Finn holds my hand as we walk into the townhouse and carefully helps me onto the couch. He waits until I get comfortable, helping me put a pillow behind my back, and then paces in front of me.

"I'm going to kill that asshole," he grinds out, clenching his fists.

I pull my hair into a ponytail. "Finn, I don't want you to get in any trouble. Hopefully, he quits."

He halts and looks at me in concern. "What if he doesn't?"

My shoulders slump. "Maybe I'll quit. His wife shouted from the rooftops that I slept with her husband without even clarifying that I'd had no idea he was a damn husband!" I'm nearly screaming at the end of my statement.

"Whatever you want to do, you have my support," he says before falling to his knees and taking my hand.

---

FINN TOOK MY MIND—WELL, *attempted* to take my mind—off what had happened today with pizza and ice cream. I could sleep for days and not forget what happened. Heck, they could try hypnotizing me, and it'd still be lodged in my brain. It's the most embarrassing moment in my life. Nothing will ever top that.

It was almost like something out of a movie—where the angry wife stomps through the workplace, confronting her cheating husband and his mistress. The only problem is, it's my real life ... and I had no idea about her. It sucks that she didn't blare out the entire story. Heck, I'm sure if she did a poll, most people would say they had no idea Gavin was married until the day she came in and introduced herself.

I wonder if that's why she made it known he was married when she got into town. It could've happened in the past, and she wanted to stop it before it did again.

My attention moves from the TV when my phone beeps with a text. I chew into my lower lip, contemplating on whether to check it. Gavin has been texting nonstop. So have my coworkers. Knowing it's for the best, I ignore it.

"Georgia texted me since she figured you're avoiding your phone," Finn says.

He holds out his phone to me, and I read her text.

**Georgia: Grace, how are you?**

I hit the reply button.

**Me: Okay, I guess. Given the situation.**

**Georgia: I set bitches straight all day. They know what a pig Gavin is and how he lied to you.**

**Me: Don't do anything stupid and get yourself fired.**

**Georgia: If that happens, we'll start a school together. Gavin is the one who needs to be fired.**

**Me: You can't get fired for sleeping with someone.**

**Georgia: Conflict of interest. He's your superior. He's been harassing you. And who knows? You might not be the only one he's done it to.**

**Me: I hope he hasn't.**

**Georgia: I'll keep my ears open. Love you.**

**Me: Love you too.**

I slump against the cushions.

Then I feel it.

Sitting straight up, I place my hand on my belly and squeal. For a moment, all my dread morphs into excitement. I wave Finn over, and he arches a brow.

"The baby!" I screech. "She just kicked." It was a slight movement, nothing too strong, but my baby is moving. In the back of my mind, I'd like to think it's her giving me a sign that everything will be okay. A reminder that it doesn't matter because I have her.

He grins. "Really?"

Grabbing his hand, I place it next to mine on my stomach. My heart beats rapidly as we wait in anticipation for another kick.

We both flinch when she kicks again.

"Hi, baby," I whisper, rubbing my stomach.

Finn beams up at me.

"We're so ready to have you here with us."

Finn falls to his knees and kisses my stomach. "We can't wait to meet you."

And just like that, my baby has already made a terrible day better.

---

WHEN FINN GETS INTO BED, I climb on top of him.

He's killed all my insecurities for being pregnant. No man has ever made me feel as beautiful as he does.

"Mmm," he groans, moving the sheet out of the way to make me more comfortable. "I like this."

He lifts me off him enough to push his shorts down, exposing his thick cock. My mouth waters. I've never been a highly sexual person, never one to talk dirty or tell someone I want them, but I love being this way with Finn.

Reaching out, his strong hand cups the back of my neck, pulling me down to his mouth. As we kiss, his hand slides down my back to my ass, cupping it while also dragging me into his erection. I love kissing this man, and I love kissing while grinding against him even more. He slips my panties to the side, causing me to buck forward, and slides a thick finger in and out of me. As I'm rocking my hips, he digs his hand into my waist to stop me and then impales me with his hard cock. I grind into him, finding the perfect position, and Finn allows me to set the rhythm. As I grow closer, my blood pressure rising, I bounce on top of him. Bending at the waist, he cups my swollen breasts, pushes them together, and drags them to his mouth. His tongue goes from one nipple to the other, back and forth, until I'm grinding so hard against him that I know I'll be sore tomorrow.

An intense burst of pleasure blasts through me, and I cry out his name before collapsing onto his chest.

"That's it, baby," Finn grunts. "I love when you come all over my cock."

I lie limp against him as he starts fucking me—really fucking me. Anchoring his hands to my hips, he holds them down while pounding into me. I struggle to catch my breath and dig my nails into his arms until he's the one moaning my name. His body shakes, and he cups my head as he joins me post-orgasm.

---

AFTER I RODE Finn until I could no longer move, he carefully helped me off him, kissed me, and rolled out of bed. Seconds later, he returns with a wet washcloth to clean me up. It's one of my favorite things he does after sex. No one knows how to take better care of me than Finn.

After he's finished, he tosses the washcloth into the dirty

laundry, grabs me a water bottle from the kitchen, and slides back into bed with me. He's so different than other men I've been with. I'm realizing now what Georgia meant all the times she said it was different when you had sex with *a real man*. None of the guys I was with before Finn were anything like this. They normally cared about their orgasms above mine and never made sure I was comfortable or cleaned up after. They typically rolled over and told me good night. Not that I've had many sexual partners since I don't like people knowing my secret.

I move to my side, staring at him, and lightly brush my fingers along the tattooed quote on his side.

It's his favorite Stephen King quote from *The Dark Tower* series. When I asked why he got it, he told me that it's the only book series he's read through and the realest quote he's ever read. I never thought too much into it, but as he revealed his past to me, I understand. Finn has gone without love for most of his life. Sure, our friends are there for him, but he's never had someone care about him more than themselves or have someone's life be consumed with their feelings for him.

That's me.

I want to show Finn that love can beat out the hate he had while growing up.

I want to prove to him it doesn't have to be destructive, though.

Our love can bring us both happiness.

# CHAPTER THIRTY-THREE

## *Finn*

THIS GAVIN MOTHERFUCKER had better count his days.

Had I not been trying to be a better man for Grace—and not wanting her to get fired from her job—I'd have already been in his office, punching his face in. He texted Grace nonstop, and she wouldn't let me reply. He said he was in love with her, would fight for their baby, and would make sure he had his parental rights.

His baby.

*Fuck that motherfucker.*

My throat grew thick as she read the texts to me. As much as I think Grace wouldn't go back to that asshole, the nerves are still there.

*What if I lose them?*

What if Grace decides she wants her baby to have a real family and that I'm no longer needed?

I shudder, pissed at myself for having those thoughts. But now that I have Grace, I'm terrified to lose her.

When Grace falls asleep, I slide out of bed and plod into the kitchen for a drink. My plan was to get a glass of water, but I opt for whiskey instead. I expel long breaths between gulps before pouring myself another while collapsing onto a chair at the table. I'm not sure how long I sit there, playing those texts back through my mind as if it were a song stuck on repeat.

I have everything I've ever wanted.

Now, there's a threat that could take it all away.

I can't lose Grace.

# CHAPTER THIRTY-FOUR

# Grace

I REFUSE to sit back and let Gavin ruin my job.

Not only do these pregnancy hormones make me break out in tears over a damn Pampers commercial, but they also bring out the anger inside me as well. Gavin needs to be the one to go. Not me. I love this job, this school, the staff—minus him—and I'm not giving it up.

Georgia texted me this morning and said Gavin took a sick day.

*Thank God.*

*I don't want to face him yet.*

The teachers' lounge turns dead silent when I walk in. Rachelle drops her bagel. The gym teacher spits out his water. The librarian nudges another teacher and signals toward me.

Georgia is behind me, always having my back. She even threatened to accidentally spill her iced coffee on someone if they said something rude.

I tend to be the shy girl and never get into confrontations. I'm the quiet one in our group of friends, but I'm done with being quiet. This is a situation I have to be loud about. I have to stick up for myself and tell people the truth.

I get straight to the point. "Did Principal Long tell any of you he was married before his wife moved here?"

People shake their heads.

Others look around the room as our coworkers answer.

"The first day he was here, he wasn't wearing a wedding ring," one girl chimes in. "Laura and I checked because we thought he was hot. When Laura asked if he was available, he smirked and never said anything else."

"Same here." A girl raises her hand. "I was shocked when I found out he was married. We joked about him having a double life."

If only I'd been a part of that conversation.

"He even told me he was on some dating website," a guy added. "When I told him I was married, he told me he was sorry."

"Ew," Georgia says.

Hearing them say this is a relief. People will believe me.

I stand up straight as if I'm about to deliver an important speech. "He told me he was single." Even though that's all I planned to say, I continue, needing them to know I'm not a shitty homewrecker, "He was staying in a temporary small condo and had no evidence of a family. We decided to keep our relationship private in fear of being the talk of the school, not because we were having an affair."

*There.*

They can choose to trust me or not.

But that's my truth, and if anyone knows me, they know I'm not a liar.

"We get it, girl," Rachelle says. "No judgment here. After all the lies he told, after the way he reacted to that other man visiting you, I'm on your side."

SOMETIMES, I forget Finn isn't the actual father of my unborn child.

Like today, as we're leaving our birthing class and stopping at Twisted Fox for dinner.

Finn is the perfect labor practice partner. He performs our breathing exercises like a pro.

Everyone greets us as if we were celebrities when we walk into the bar. With all the drama, appointments, and planning for the baby, we haven't spent as much time here as usual. Not to mention, Finn now works full-time at the dealership. We're both usually exhausted when we get home from work. Hopefully, when everything dies down, we can visit more.

When we sit down, my mind wanders.

*Will Finn be with me in the delivery room?*

If not, these classes are pointless.

*Will anyone be in there with me?*

I can ask my mom and Faith. They wouldn't say no. I'm sure Georgia and Lola would also be there for me if I needed them. As much as I love them, I feel as if I've gone through this journey with Finn more than anyone. He's the one who holds my hair back when I'm puking. The one who taped one of the ultrasound pictures onto his car dashboard.

"Everything okay?" Finn asks, staring at me from across the table—most likely picking up on my mood change.

"Yeah," I quickly reply.

"Babe," he deadpans, "I know when something is wrong, and *something is wrong*."

I don't want to have this conversation here.

I need to figure out the best way to approach it before we have it, period.

I rub my stomach. "I think the pregnancy nerves are getting to me."

"Anything I can do to help?"

That's Finn.

*What can he do to help?*

"Hey, guys!" Cassidy says, appearing at our table in her waitress outfit with a pen and notepad in her hand. "What can I grab you?"

I order a grilled cheese and lemonade. Finn orders wings and a water. Cassidy salutes us and skips off to her next table—a group of guys sporting college sports gear.

Finn leans in, resting his elbows on the table, and taps my head. "What's going on in there, baby?"

I gulp, wishing Cassidy had dropped off my lemonade already. "I'm wondering what it'll be like in labor."

"Are you nervous?"

I nod repeatedly. "Definitely nervous."

He smirks, pulling back to smack his hand against his chest in pride. "I mean, you do have the best goddamn birthing coach in the world. I'm expected to *tap in*."

"I can't believe you just referred to being in the delivery room as *tapping in*."

"As I told you before, I'm here for whatever you need. A shoulder to cry on during *Vampire Diaries*, hands to rub your sore feet, setting up the nursery, there with you when the baby is born. I'm all yours. In fact, it'd be an honor to be there with you in the room ... if you'll have me."

I grin wildly. "I'd absolutely love that."

Cassidy drops off our drinks, and minutes later, Silas and Georgia join us. They want all the baby updates. Georgia asks Finn if he's ready for the baby to come as if he really were the father. It seems our friends are on the same thought process as I am.

It's us.

Me and Finn doing this together.

I need to stop thinking otherwise.

I need to stop worrying about everything falling apart.
Becoming a mess.
Only that's exactly what happens.

## CHAPTER THIRTY-FIVE

# Finn

MY LOUD-ASS RINGTONE shakes me out of my sleep.

Nearly knocking down everything on the nightstand, I quickly grab my phone and silence it, not wanting to wake Grace. There's no stopping the frown from forming when I see the name flashing across the screen. He'll keep calling until I answer, especially when it's this late.

Calls this late are never a good thing.

Like I told Grace, I'm always on pins and needles, waiting for the call to hear I no longer have a father. He might not be the best father, but he's my father, goddammit. Albeit a shitty one, he's the only family member I had growing up. My grandparents nor his siblings wanted anything to do with us. My mother was gone. We were all each other had. My father could've given me up when he and my mother couldn't provide for me. He could've said *fuck that* to having a child and sent me to foster care, but he didn't.

I'll forever be grateful for that, so maybe that's why I answer when I shouldn't.

Why I give him money when I shouldn't.

Why I stupidly see him doing his fucking job as a father as a favor to me.

Like I owe him for my life when he's the one who chose to bring me into it.

Pulling on a pair of gym shorts, I silence the phone when it rings again and rush into the living room. Just as I'm about to call him back, my phone rings again.

"Hello?" I answer in a harsh whisper.

"Finn," my father barks out, "I'm stranded, and I need a ride home."

"Stranded?" I hiss, stumbling toward the laundry room and picking up a dirty tee. I sniff it, finding it satisfactory, and slip it on. The least amount of movements to wake up Grace, the better. "How are you stranded somewhere? You have a car."

"I hitched a ride with some old friends to catch up with buddies from high school. Good ole times, you know?"

"Can whoever you rode with take you home?"

"I can't find one ... and the other is wasted off his ass." He snort-laughs as if it's the funniest shit he's heard all night.

"I'll call you a taxi or Uber."

"I ain't getting in no Uber and getting murdered!" he drunkenly screeches. "You want to be planning my funeral, kid?"

I snatch my keys, shove my feet into my shoes, and turn off the alarm. "Send me the address, and I'll pick you up."

---

THERE'S NOT a doubt in my mind that it's a drug house I'm pulling up to.

Snatching my phone from the cupholder, I call my dad, but he doesn't answer. I curse before calling him again. No answer. Sitting in my car, I debate on leaving his ungrateful ass, but knowing I'd probably have to return later, I get out of the car. Old '80s rock blares from the house as I walk inside, a cloud of smoke hitting me in the face. Places like this always make me anxious. The police could show up at any time and think I'm involved with whatever bullshit is happening here.

This isn't the first time I've had to pick him up from a hell-hole like this. I've made it clear to my father that he's not to call me for bail money if he gets arrested. I blink a few times, clearing my vision, and continue walking until I arrive in the living room. A crowd of people, my dad among them, are sitting in the living room, drinking ... and doing other illegal shit.

"In my car *now*," I yell to my father. "You have thirty goddamn seconds to get your ass up, or you won't have a ride home. You can stay in this dump."

"Hey, man," a guy sporting circular glasses cries out. "That's fucking rude."

I ignore the man and keep my eyes on my father.

"My son, always the buzzkill," he says, pulling himself up from the couch with a beer in his hand. "Always tryna tell me what to do, like he's my parent."

"If you acted like the parent, I wouldn't have to." My blood pressure rises with every word that leaves my mouth.

This shit can't happen when the baby is born.

I won't keep enabling my father.

*No more.*

"You shut it," he yells. "I was your father when no one else was there to take care of you."

*Oh fuck. Here comes the emotional drunk.*

I grab the back of his shirt, jerking him forward, and push him outside. "You're mistaken. I took care of you. Who kept food in the house? Me. Who made sure I had everything I needed for school? Me. Who paid when the landlord came knocking on the door for late rent? Me."

He stumbles forward and turns to look at me, snarling, "You shut your mouth! I sacrificed a lot for you too."

I point at my car. "Get your ass in there before I make you walk home."

He screams profanities while stomping to the car and slams the door shut. When I slide into the driver's side, I shake my head in frustration. The ride back to my apartment is quiet. He's still crashing there, and since I've been so busy, I haven't pushed the issue for him to move out. I check on him regularly, and as far as I can tell, he hasn't been doing stupid shit inside it.

"Thanks for the ride," he grumbles, shooting me a quick glance of what looks like ... gratitude?

*That's a first.*

I nod and wait until he disappears inside the apartment before fishing my phone from my pocket. My stomach twists when I see the messages, one after the other after the other. Eight texts from Grace, asking me to call her and where I am, and ten calls. Hitting her name, I put my phone on speaker and race home.

No answer.

I call again.

No answer.

I call Faith next.

"Grace!" I yell into the speaker when Faith answers. "I had to run an errand. She called and texted me a shit ton of times, and now, she's not answering."

"Where are you?" Faith's voice is panicked, making me grow more alarmed alongside her.

"On my way home." I speed around a car, hearing them blare their horn behind me, and hurriedly beat a yellow light before it turns red. I hear rustling in the background.

"She's probably freaking out," Faith mutters, and I'm not sure if it's something she wanted me to hear.

"What?" I yell. "Why would she be freaking out?"

*Because I'm gone?*

*Because I left in the middle of the night?*

I know her ex was a cheater, so maybe she thinks I left to be with another woman?

Faith blows out a ragged breath. "It's a long story. Just hurry up and get there."

"I'm working on it," I grind out, tightening my hold on the steering wheel.

Luckily, it doesn't take long before I'm pulling back into the driveway. I jump out of my car and sprint toward the house. I'm yelling Grace's name as I burst inside. Every light in the house is on, shining bright. When I turn the corner and hit the living room, I find Grace pacing back and forth. Her body is shaking, and when she turns to look at me, her face is red. Tears run down her splotchy cheeks. She's staring at me, but her eyes are blank, vacant, as if she's almost in a trance.

I bolt toward her and yell her name. Her hands are shaking when I grab them to stop her. She freezes, blinking at me, but doesn't say a word. Every muscle in her body trembles as I hold her, and her crying breaks out into sobs.

Pulling her against my chest, I hold her tight. "Calm down, baby. What happened?"

"They ..."

My body tightens at that one word, and I pull away.

"They came in and tried to hurt her!" she shrills, painfully staring at me before retreating backward.

"Came where?" I scope out our surroundings, searching for someone. When Grace doesn't reply, I stalk out of the living room and down the hallway. "Are they in here? Did they leave? Did you call the goddamn cops?"

All I see is red as I charge through the house, frantically checking the kitchen, bedrooms, bathrooms, closets for someone but find nothing.

Grace is muttering, "No," under her breath as she follows me.

I whip around and snap my fingers in front of her face. She blinks at me as if struggling to process what's happening.

"I shot them," she rambles before hysterically repeating, "I shot them," over and over again.

She's hysterical. I struggle to find words. Struggle to figure out what the hell to do.

"You shot someone?" I ask, attempting to calm my voice in hopes that it'll calm her. "Where are they?" My eyes widen. "Where the hell did you even get a gun?" My gaze stupidly darts around the room again, just in case I missed a dead body lying around here somewhere.

"Grace!"

With Grace still in my hold, I turn us to find Faith rushing into the townhome. Her hand flies to her mouth as she takes in Grace's appearance.

"What is going on?" I scream, my voice shaking. "She said she fucking shot someone!"

Faith stumbles toward us but still remains a few inches away. "She's having an episode."

My heart pounds against my chest as confusion overwhelms me. "An episode?"

# CHAPTER THIRTY-SIX

# Grace

I'M SITTING cross-legged on the couch where Finn and Faith walked me to and sat me down. Finn is on his knees in front of me. My eyesight is blurry as I stare at him, fighting to focus on his gorgeous face, but it's a struggle. He's speaking, snapping his fingers in front of my face. I open my mouth, but no words form.

I fixate on Finn in distress. His skin is bunched around his eyes as he speaks to me. My ears are ringing, and I can't hear him or read his lips.

I'm burning up, my body temperature feeling close to a fever. Torment overcomes me before I suddenly jerk out of my daze. When I bounce back into reality, I cringe, wishing I could sink into the cushions and disappear. As I focus on the room, those around me realize I've returned to the real world. Finn flings his arms around my shoulders and pulls me into his chest, shielding me.

"Baby," he whispers as I fall limp in his hold. "Talk to me."

Staring over his shoulder, I cast a glance to Faith and nod.

"Thank God," she breathes out. She hastily steps forward

before stopping. Normally, this is the part when she grabs me, hugging me tight like Finn is.

Finn knew what I needed.

Just like Faith knows.

I've had attacks in front of others before.

Georgia, who called my parents and did her best to console me. Luckily, with us being friends for so long, she was aware.

My parents, who know how to handle me.

And an ex, who lost his shit and told me I was crazy. He's most likely the one who gave me anxiety about my issues coming to light.

I don't want to be *crazy*. I don't want to be afraid of the dark anymore.

I cry into Finn's shoulder, soaking his shirt, but he doesn't flinch. Faith sits next to me and rubs my shoulder in tiny circles.

I should feel stupid. I normally do.

Stupid, crazy, and frightened.

But at this moment, I don't.

I feel loved. Understood. Safe.

The only sounds in the room are my sobs as I break down and Faith saying, "It'll be okay."

I'm unsure of how much time passes as we sit like this—me clinging on to Finn like he's my lifeline and Faith sitting beside me, comforting me, like always. They both allow me to release the fear I'm experiencing while they shelter me from panicking further. My crying calms, and hiccups replace the tears.

The humiliation I had ceases as I realize the people around me won't judge me. They love me—every quirk, flaw, and fear. When I pull away from Finn, his focus doesn't leave my face. His wide eyes study me, inspecting every inch of me as if he's searching for answers he's too scared to ask.

"Grace, honey." My sister's words come out slow and cautious.

I flick away tears with my hand and look over at her.

She clasps her hand over mine—a silent question, asking if I'm okay.

"I'm good now," I croak out. "I'm good now."

Finn, who seemed almost speechless, finally says, "Is there anything I can do?"

"No." I sniffle. "You guys being here is all I need."

These types of situations aren't easy.

Dating someone like me is difficult.

I'm more than what's on the outside. My webs are weaved thick to keep things hidden.

I can't sleep alone at night.

I'm practically afraid of the dark.

I don't trust people.

I'm a hot mess, but I mask it well.

"Do you want me to stay?" Faith asks.

I shake my head. "No. I'm okay."

Finn is here.

Faith squeezes my hand. "You sure?"

"I'm sure." I gulp and look at Finn. "I just want to go to bed and sleep this off."

"All right," Finn says.

Faith stands at the same time Finn helps me up from the couch. She hugs me tight, kisses me on the cheek, and tells me to call her if I need anything.

I wait until she leaves, surprised my body isn't trembling.

*Will Finn ask questions now that we're alone?*

"Can you just take me to bed, and we'll talk tomorrow?" I ask before he gets a chance to interrogate me on my freak-out.

Finn nods. "Of course."

As he walks us to the bedroom, I'm squeezing his hand so tight that I'm surprised I don't cut off circulation. He flips on the light as if knowing that's what I need and tightly tucks me into bed. Without a word and without bothering to turn off the light, he slips into bed beside me and drags me to his chest.

"I got you," he whispers into my ear. "I'm here."

I shut my eyes, positive I'll be fighting sleep all night.

I'm wrong.

Being in Finn's arms is the relaxant I need.

I fall asleep moments later.

THE NEXT DAY, I call off of work, go back to sleep, and don't wake up until I'm no longer exhausted.

Last night mentally drained me.

That stress isn't good for me or the baby.

I wanted to break down and cry again when Finn told me he called in too. Knowing my sister, she told Brian about last night. He'd have no issue with giving Finn time off to be with me. I'm grateful Faith found someone who understands the trauma we went through. Throughout their relationship, he's always been her helping hand. Her savior.

I'm sipping on the fruit smoothie Finn made me and lounging on the couch. The news plays on the TV, but I'm numb to whatever the anchor is saying. All my brain is processing is how I'll need to explain myself to Finn. After what happened last night, it can't be pushed underneath the rug. I wanted to hide it from him for as long as I could, but I know it's finally time. Like Brian is for Faith, Finn can be my savior.

Finn sits next to me. His smoothie is greener than mine. He makes fun of my smoothies and how I only add four spinach leaves but refer to them as *green smoothies* sometimes.

"It's better than eating a cheeseburger," is my argument.

So throw in all the fruits and give me something yummy.

"Whenever you're ready to talk, I'm here," Finn tells me.

My thoughts rush back to when Faith told me she confided

in Brian about what had happened to us. She drank nearly a bottle of wine to prepare herself and cried the entire time. He held her, and in the end, she said it was the best thing she'd ever done. She no longer had to hide behind her fears, as we'd done for years. Now, she's happily married with a daughter, and she can sleep without a night-light. No more nightmares. No more flashbacks. I want that too.

In order to get that, I have to put on my big-girl panties like Faith did and open myself up. Unfortunately, I can't chug a bottle of wine. *A smoothie it is.* Maybe I should throw a Kit Kat in with it—you know, for stress-relief purposes.

I sit cross-legged—my favorite position for talking about uncomfortable situations. It's almost like I'm in my own anxiety ball.

*This needs to be done.*

*I trust Finn enough to confide in him.*

*I love him.*

Snagging the remote from the coffee table, I turn off the TV. Shifting to face him, I blow out a raspy breath. Noticing the change in mood, Finn settles his smoothie on the end table next to him and provides me with his full attention.

Before I bare myself to him, I take in the sight of him. His eyes are tired. The few times I woke up last night, Finn was awake. Exhaustion registered on his face when he kissed me good morning and helped me into the shower. Last night seemed to mentally suck him dry as well.

I hug myself, and though it's a struggle, I meet Finn's eyes. Other than the police and my parents, Georgia is the only person I've revealed my skeletons to. Lola knows bits and pieces, but not the entire story.

"When I was thirteen, two men broke into our house," I start, wetting my lips. "My parents were at some charity event that Faith and I had begged them to stay home from. The guys were family members of a criminal my father had given a harsh but deserving sentence to. The men came for retribution—to pay my father back for not giving their brother only a slap on the wrist." My body suddenly feels ten times heavier. "I was in my bedroom upstairs when Faith screamed. I ran out and looked over the stairwell, seeing them pinning Faith down. They told her she was going to pay for what my father had done. In fear, I ran to my parents' bedroom and grabbed the gun from my father's nightstand. I sprinted down the stairs ... and they were ..." I gulp, and the tears I begged to stay away appear. "They were about to rape her. I yelled for them to stop or I'd blow their heads off. The man laughed and lunged for the gun, so I shot him."

Finn is quiet, watching me with intent.

I breathe in deeply before slowly exhaling. "I figured shooting the guy would stop the man on top of Faith, but it only seemed to anger him more. She was lying there, crying and screaming, so ... I shot him in the back. He fell limply on Faith's body, causing her to scream louder. She shoved him off her and slid across the floor before gaining the ability to walk. She scrambled away from him and into my arms. She yelled at me to call 911, but all I could do was stare at the guy squirming on the floor. Tears were in his eyes. I knew I should help him, but I was so angry. Faith ran into the living room to grab her phone as I watched the men I had just shot, lying there and bleeding, without helping them. My counselor said I was frozen in trauma, but after all these years, I'm still not sure why I didn't try to help them.

I scrub a hand over my wet face. "The guy who was on top of Faith wound up dying. The other had surgery and lived." My chest tightens as if it were strangling the words out of me. "I killed someone, Finn, and what happened that night haunts me. I have nightmares, replaying them barging into our home. I'm scared of being home alone at night. I live in constant fear of it happening again."

It made the news, and my parents moved us to Anchor Ridge, a few towns over, so we weren't the talk of the neighborhood. There were mixed emotions on what'd happened—some people praised us for sticking up for ourselves while others were angry a thirteen-year-old knew how to shoot a man. They called my father irresponsible for having loaded weapons in the house. Little did they know, he'd taken us to gun safety classes, almost as if he knew there was a risk it'd happen with his job.

I'm in tears by the time I'm finished. "I don't want to be this way ... to be broken." I press my hand to my chest. "I'm about to be a mother. It'll be my job to protect my baby, so I need to stop being scared."

"Last night," Finn says in a low tone, "what happened?"

"I woke up, and you being gone must've triggered something in me."

He slowly scoots closer, waiting for me to tell him it's okay to do so. I sluggishly nod, and he pulls me onto his lap. Like last night, he holds me close and allows me to release my hurt against his chest. When I drag myself away, a gentle smile is on his face.

He plays with a strand of my hair, twirling it around his thick finger. "You're always safe with me, baby." He dips his chin slightly. "My father needed a ride home, and I didn't want to wake you. It won't happen again." He drops a kiss onto my lips, then my nose, and then my forehead. "Thank you for telling me this. It means everything to me."

# CHAPTER THIRTY-SEVEN

## GRACE

# *Grace*

"IT'S ABOUT GODDAMN TIME," Silas says when Finn and I walk into Lincoln's penthouse, holding hands.

"Another couple," Lincoln adds with a smirk. "Four down." He casts a glance at Silas. "One to go."

Silas flips him off.

The reactions aren't surprising. Not all of our friends knew about Finn's and my change in relationship, although I'm sure they already assumed with us living together. But we haven't been around as much, given the current drama, my pregnancy, and him no longer working at Twisted Fox.

The girls knew after finding out what happened with Gavin's wife. They were adamant about coming over for a girls' night. They asked questions. Questions I couldn't lie about.

It's been a long week. There's been an ease in my nerves since Gavin took a leave from work—most likely waiting for talk of his wife's actions to die down. Even though I set everyone straight, I've steered clear of the teachers' lounge.

According to Georgia, after I left on the day Gavin's wife confronted me, Gavin charged out of his office in search of his wife after finding out that she hadn't left. He led her out of the building, threatening to call the police with every step if she didn't listen.

I haven't decided what I'll do if he comes back. Finn said he'd support me if I quit, but I love teaching too much. I pray that Gavin stays gone until my maternity leave, and then I'll decide from there.

"I'm really happy for you," Georgia says, perking up next to me.

"Remember how we'd bet who'd get pregnant first?" Lola asks.

Georgia laughs, pointing at her. "And we all said it'd be you."

"Pfft," Cassidy says. "You thought *Lola*, the commitment-phobe, would be the first?"

"We damn sure didn't think it'd be Grace," Georgia argues. "And I wasn't about to jinx myself in high school."

I laugh. "Me neither. That's why we voted on Lola."

Lola delivers a red-lipped smile. "Come to think of it, I don't know why we didn't put our money on Grace. She's always loved kids."

"Now, who's the next to get pregnant?" Jamie bounces a cooing Isabella, her baby, on her knee. "Two down—me and Grace."

"Uh ..." Cassidy hesitates before slowly holding up her hand. "That'd be me." She inhales a quick breath before continuing. "Well ... not next since I already am."

All our attention swings to her.

"I'm sorry," she rushes out, staring at me. "I've kept quiet because I didn't want to outshine your moment. I wanted to try to find the right time to tell you ... and I guess this is the right time."

I squeal, "Really?"

She nods. "Like you, I was totally shocked."

I frown but then immediately correct myself, hating that

she thought announcing her pregnancy would ruin any moment of mine. I get it, though. She's told me plenty of stories about the competitiveness in the sorority she was in before getting expelled from college.

"I guess that makes three down," Georgia says, scooting down the couch to hug Cassidy.

"Congrats, girl." Lola blows her a kiss. "We're going to have a shit ton of baby shopping to do."

Snapping my fingers, I gesture for Georgia to help me. She jumps up from the couch, grabs my elbow, and pulls me to my feet.

Taking the few steps to Cassidy, I hug her tight. "I'm so happy for you, babe."

It's nice to have someone going on this journey with me.

She hugs me back. "Thank you. I swear, after taking the test, I understood your panic. I was freaking the hell out."

When I pull away, I take the seat next to her. "What did Lincoln say?"

"Another reason I was nervous. Our relationship is kind of new, but he's ecstatic." A relaxed grin spreads across her face. "I also wanted to talk to you about the living situation. The town-home is a two-bedroom, and you'll need a nursery. The pent-house is a two-bedroom, and we'll need a nursery. If you're okay with it, the townhouse is all yours. Jamie agrees too."

# CHAPTER THIRTY-EIGHT

# Finn

"IF GEORGIA KEEPS DRAGGING me to baby showers, I'm going to make her ass have my baby real soon," Archer grunts, leaning back in his chair.

He chose the worst timing for his comment because as soon as the words leave his mouth, Georgia passes us.

She comes to a halt. "News flash, babe: baby showers are for *everyone*." She licks her lips. "And I love the baby talk. We can practice when we get home tonight."

He throws his head back. "You'd better keep that promise."

She saunters closer, tips her head down, and smacks a kiss to Archer's lips.

Today is Grace's baby shower, and it's being held at Faith's house. The girls have been hard at work, making it perfect for Grace. It looks like a damn flamingo blew up in here with all the pink. Grace told her parents she wanted to keep it small, but there are still at least fifty people here hanging out in the backyard.

I've met Grace's grandparents, aunts, uncles, cousins, and countless other people I've forgotten the names of. Every move I make, I'm stopped and introduced as Grace's boyfriend and the father of her child. I get asked how long we've dated, when I plan to pop the question, and if I'm ready to be a father. I've repeated the same story so many goddamn times that it's hard for even me to remember it's a lie.

*I'm not the baby's father.*

*But I want to be her father.*

The dust from Gavin has started to settle. The asshole is still on leave with another principal filling in for him. The day after Cassidy moved out of the townhouse, Grace and I went shopping for the nursery. She sat on the floor, setting up her shower registry online while I painted the walls yellow and assembled the furniture.

I chuckle. "I love how she always sets you straight."

"Oh, fuck off," Archer groans. "Don't act like Grace isn't the same with you."

"Speaking of Grace, it seems like you've done a kick-ass job of convincing people you're the dad," Lincoln says, grabbing his beer and taking a long draw. "Our plan has worked."

"Yeah," Cohen says. "Do you plan to step up ... permanently?"

I gulp back my water and search the yard for Grace before replying. She's at a table with the girls, her parents, and her grandmother. She throws her head back, laughing, her tight braids falling along her shoulders. She lights up, her smile bright. I love seeing her this way, especially after everything she's gone through. She's wearing a white dress that shows off her belly with the pearl necklace I bought her for her birthday last year.

Every day when I wake up, my goal is to make Grace's day better than the last.

"If she'll have me, yes," I finally answer. "The dad is an asshole. Grace and I are together. I've been by her side, not him, and we plan to raise her together."

We've talked about it countless times. When we sit on the

bed, feeling her stomach, waiting for the baby to kick. When we're on the couch, our favorite show playing in the background, listening to the baby's heartbeat with the machine we bought. I've gone to every doctor's appointment since the ultrasound and all her labor classes.

Cohen slaps me on the back. "I'm happy for you, brother. I've known Grace since she and Georgia became best friends. I've never seen her as happy with someone as she is with you."

"Cheers to our relationships and babies!" Lincoln says, holding up his beer.

"I'll cheers to babies because you're my friends, but fuck no to a relationship cheers," Silas mutters.

"Way to put a damper on a good day," Lincoln comments.

"Don't mind him," Archer says, waving his hand through the air. "He's pissed Lola is dating his brother."

"First off, he's not my brother," Silas corrects. "And second, she's not dating him. They went out to dinner. I told her not to. She's not listening to me." He says the last sentence with a twisted snarl.

Archer levels his eyes on Silas. "Man, unless you stop bullshitting and date her, she'll continue not to listen to you."

Our conversation is interrupted by Grace's mom yelling that it's time to cut the cake.

"Finn!" she says, calling me over with a wave of her hand. "Come on!"

Standing, I walk to the front of the yard and meet Grace at a long table. A three-layer pink cake sits alongside endless desserts—again, all pink. We stand at the head of it, on display, and I kiss Grace without even thinking about the crowd.

Everyone applauds, and when I pull away, a flush runs up her cheeks.

"I'm pretty sure the inside of that cake will be pink," Grace whispers to me.

I raise a brow. "Let's see, shall we?"

She grips the cake slicer, and my hand cradles hers.

Just as we're about to slice the cake, there's a loud clapping, followed by a deep, taunting voice saying, "Sorry for running late."

Terror flashes in Grace's eyes, and mine blaze with fury as Gavin strolls through the yard as if he owns the place. She drops the cake cutter, and it tumbles to the ground.

Gavin stands tall and smirks while staring straight at me. "I know it looks bad for the father, but traffic was a bitch."

# CHAPTER THIRTY-NINE

# Grace

THIS CAN'T BE HAPPENING.

Gavin makes a beeline in my direction, and my anxiety worsens the closer he gets. The smirk on his face confirms he's not here to do the right thing. He's here looking for trouble. This is about to be a god-awful mess. He walks as if he were leading a parade, and this is one big show.

My grandmother's wrinkled hand flies to her chest as she gasps.

My mother's drink drops from her hand at the same speed my heart feels like it's dropping from my chest.

My father says, "What the hell?"

"I'm going to kill that motherfucker," Finn growls.

People speak around me—some in hushed voices, some stating their concern loud enough that I can hear.

*What the heck do I do?*

I look at Finn, who appears to be on the same thinking page as me. He can charge across the yard and beat up Gavin, but that'd make him look bad in front of my family and friends. I gaze furtively around the yard, and everyone's attention is on the shit show about to start.

"Why is he here?" Finn seethes, his nostrils flaring.

"I-I have no idea," I stutter.

As far as I knew, Gavin was still on leave. He hasn't texted or called in weeks. Someone even mentioned they heard his wife was making them move back to their hometown.

Gavin turns in a circle before pointing at Finn. "This guy here, he's a fraud." He gestures to the crowd. "They are deceiving all of you. I am Grace's baby's father, but Grace got mad at me. Now, this guy is stepping in. But I'm going to fight for my baby."

Finn must lose all patience because this is the moment he charges toward Gavin. He gets one punch in, causing Gavin to stumble back before Archer snags Finn around the waist and pulls him back. Considering Finn's and Gavin's size difference, Gavin is stupid to taunt Finn. He'd better feel lucky that Archer stopped them.

I stand frozen in place, unsure of what to do.

"You need to leave," Archer warns Gavin, still holding Finn back.

Gavin wipes the blood off his lip. "I'm not going anywhere until Grace tells the truth."

"You have thirty seconds to turn your ass around, or I'm letting him get another punch in."

Everyone awaits Gavin's next move since he's the star of the show.

I'm brought into a hug, and I cast a glance at Georgia as she takes me into her hold. My sister comes along the other side, doing the same thing. Lola, Cassidy, and Jamie join us. Behind Finn are Cohen, Silas, Brian, and Lincoln. Gavin would be stupid not to leave because the sight of all of them together, pissed off, is terrifying.

"If he doesn't listen to Archer, I am taking this cake and throwing it at his head," Georgia says. "I'll buy you another one."

"Then I'm kicking him in the balls," Lola says.

"And I'll pour my drink over his head," Faith adds.

Gavin and Finn face off, glaring at each other, and Gavin doesn't budge.

Brian steps in, walking in front of Archer to speak to Gavin. "Look, this is my home. I'm asking you to leave. Otherwise, I'll call the police and have them escort you off my property." Brian fishes his phone from his pocket and holds it up. "I'm sure a police report would prevent you from securing any job in your field in the future. Think about that."

Reality dawns on Gavin as if that thought never crossed his dumbass brain.

He jerks his head toward me. "You need to tell them the truth because, in the end, I'll be there for you and the baby."

I pull away from my friends and bolt in Gavin's direction. Finn tries to stop me as I circle around them to get into his face, but I swat him away.

"Don't you get it, Gavin?" My tone is consumed with anguish, and my heart shudders in my chest as my tears come. "I want nothing to do with you." I swing my arm toward Finn. "This man here, he was the one who picked up all the responsibility you didn't."

Talking comes from everyone again at my confession.

"He was there for me at my appointments," I continue. "He's already providing for the baby, buying everything she'll need—"

"She?" Gavin's eyes widen, and he flinches while retreating a step. "You're having a girl?"

I ignore his question and go on, hoping my words sink in, and he never comes back. "He takes care of me, and goddammit, he's not married!"

That's when the reaction from the crowd goes ballistic in shock. I've never felt as on display in my life.

Gavin cowers, and his eyes bore into mine. "When he leaves

you—because you know he will—you'll regret pushing me out of your life."

"Not fucking happening," Finn scoffs.

"He's not like you and me," Gavin says. "A man like that doesn't go for sweet girls, Grace, baby. You'll bore him, and he'll run off with someone else."

"You motherfucker!" Finn breaks from Archer, but Brian scurries to stand in front of Gavin, protecting him from a beatdown.

"Whatever happens, happens." I play it off as if his words didn't hurt me, but my chin trembles and more tears appear. "I'd rather be a single mom than be with you."

Brian pushes Gavin back. "The cops"—another push—"will be here any minute"—another push—"so go."

Gavin solemnly nods, finally getting the hint, and he turns and walks away.

Finn rushes to my side and pulls me against his chest.

"Get me out of here," I say, finally allowing the tears to break free.

"I got you."

He cradles my head into his chest as he walks me into Faith's house. We pass a few people sitting in the dining room, and he takes me upstairs to their open guest bedroom. He shuts the door, carefully sits me on the bed, and falls to his knees, so our faces are level with each other's.

My chin quivers as he stares at me with pain in his eyes.

"Baby," he croaks out, nearly in tears himself, "I am so sorry."

I run my hands through his soft hair. "That wasn't your fault."

It was mine.

I'm the one who allowed Gavin into my life.

Who slept with him.

*How did he even know where to find me?*

*The details of my baby shower?*

"When something painful happens to you, it hurts me too," Finn says, taking my hand in his. "And all that bullshit he said about me getting bored with you? That'll never happen."

My hands fall when he leans forward to press his lips to mine.

"I love you, Grace, and we'll figure this out."

Our attention turns away from each other at a knock on the door. It slowly opens, and my mother and Faith stand in the doorway. My mother's eyes are red and glistening with tears as she scurries into the bedroom.

"Oh, honey," she cries out, falling onto her knees next to Finn. "Is that true? What that asshole said?"

I can't help but chuckle at her reference to Gavin.

I nod. "It's true. We started dating, but then I found out he was married."

My mom sighs.

"I told him it was over, but then later, I found out I was pregnant," I confide. "I thought I'd have to do it alone, but Finn stepped up." I cast a glance at Finn. "We're in love, and we plan to raise the baby together."

"We will," Finn says. "I don't care if we have to fight him tooth and nail in court."

"We'll figure out a way for that to happen," Faith says. "You have a family who works in law."

I wipe my eyes. "What am I supposed to do about everyone out there? I can't go back out. I'm humiliated."

It'll be rude, but there's no way I can face everyone after what Gavin did. I'm already going to be the gossip for the next year and considered a joke. I lied to everyone about who the father of my baby is. Then he, the biological father, showed up and turned out to be a giant asshole, and while I confronted him, I aired that he was married.

*Oh, what a baby shower to remember.*

## CHAPTER FORTY

---

# *Finn*

I HOLD my head high as I thank everyone for coming after telling Grace I'd take care of the people at the baby shower. I'm embarrassed as fuck, but I can't imagine the humiliation she's going through. A few ask questions before leaving, to which I give them quick one-worded answers. Others thank me for being there for Grace. No one has said anything negative ... to my face, at least. I'm sure there will be tons of talk about this later.

I have a shit ton of stuff to figure out.

*How did Gavin find out about Grace's baby shower?*

*How can I get him to leave us the fuck alone?*

Brian helps me see people out while the girls are with Grace.

"Thank you."

I glance over to see Gregory stopping next to me.

I raise a brow. "What?"

"Thank you." He holds out his hand, and I shake it. "I was worried about you and my daughter—not going to lie. Tyra and I thought it was too fast. We were upset we'd never met you ... well, met you as our daughter's boyfriend. It was strange to us, but we didn't know to think otherwise. What you did for Grace, being that hand for her to hold, means a lot to me. I'm sure playing the part was largely so Grace didn't disappoint us. As far as I see it, you're the father. A father is more than genes. A father is someone who will do anything for his child, who is there for them through thick and thin, and that, Finn, is you. I'm honored to have you as part of our family."

Their acceptance means so much to me. There's only one thing holding Grace and me back from being a family, and I need to correct that.

---

IT WASN'T hard to find Gavin's address.

I just asked Georgia, the detective. All she needs is the internet, and she can find anything about anyone in minutes. Pulling up to the two-story home he recently moved into with his wife, I think twice if this is the right plan. It could result in doing more harm than good, but I need to take my chances. If there's a way I can get Gavin out of the picture, I'll take it. If it ends up going bad, I'll deal with the consequences.

Exhaling a deep breath, I step out of my car and stroll up the walkway. Three days have passed since the baby shower disaster, and Grace and I have worked on devising a plan to get rid of Gavin.

The door is answered within minutes after I ring the doorbell, and a dark-haired pregnant woman stands in front of me.

I lean back on my heels. "I'm looking for Gavin."

She tilts her head to the side. "Who are you?"

"I'm a friend."

"Gavin doesn't have friends here." She shakes her head. "Well ... male friends."

I can't stop myself from snarling at her response. "Look, I need to talk to him. Is he home?"

She doesn't move.

Since being vague isn't working, I go for lying next. "It's about his job."

Her shoulders straighten. "What about it?"

"Vivica, that's Grace's boyfriend."

Vivica whips around, and Gavin stands a few feet away from her, his eyes narrowed in my direction. She goes to slam the door in my face, but I dart my hand out to stop her.

I lower my voice. "I promise, this is only to help you. Hear me out."

Gavin doesn't say a word, just delivers a dirty look as I walk in. I can't decipher whether he is only allowing this to keep from pissing off his wife or if he's truly interested in why I'm here. We pass two kids playing in the living room, and Vivica asks them to go play in their bedrooms.

Gavin stands straight, clasping his hands in front of him. "To what do we owe the pleasure, Finn?"

"I want you to stay away from Grace," I demand.

"What are you talking about?" Vivica asks. "He told me he hasn't talked to her since he took his leave."

"That's a lie." I scratch my head and put all my attention on Vivica. "He showed up at her baby shower, causing a scene and telling everyone he was going to fight for his rights as the baby's father."

Vivica takes a step forward. "Excuse me?" She whips back to glare at Gavin. "Is this true?"

"I ..." Gavin stutters for the right words. "We were in an argument ... and I was ... just trying to figure out what to do."

"How did you even know where her shower was?" I ask.

He shrugs. "I still talk to a few teachers, and they overheard Grace and Georgia discussing it. They also invited some coworkers, and I got my hands on an invite."

"You bastard!" Vivica slaps Gavin across the face, doing the work I wish I could, but I'm trying to stay out of trouble. "You promised me you'd stay away from her! You swore to quit pulling this stuff and finally be faithful." She rubs her stomach. "We're having another baby, for Christ's sake!" she cries out. "You're destroying our family."

"I'm sorry!" Gavin croaks. "I'm trying to do better. I promise."

"You showing up at my girlfriend's baby shower isn't trying to do better," I argue. "It's you doing worse." I step forward. "You want to make things right with your wife ... with your family? Leave mine alone."

"Is she okay with that?" Vivica asks. "She doesn't expect anything from Gavin?"

I shake my head. "Not one damn thing."

"Looks like yet another lie," Vivica says, words directed at Gavin. "You told me she is suing you for child support and won't let you get out of this."

"Not true." My attention is also on Gavin as I pull out the envelope from my back pocket. "I can make it easy for you to fix your marriage." I open the envelope and slap the papers against his chest. "Here are papers to sign over any rights you'd have to Grace's baby. We will pay you ten thousand dollars to get you the fuck out of our hair." My gaze swings to Vivica. "We won't ask you for a dime, and you won't have to worry about any extra baby-mama drama."

Being the kick-ass attorney she is, Faith drew up papers and went through all the legalities with us on possible scenarios to get Gavin out of the picture. Grace's parents offered the ten thousand in hopes it'd convince Gavin further. I'm grateful as fuck for everything they're doing for us.

Vivica snatches the papers and quickly scans them before shoving them into Gavin's chest the same way I had. "Sign the papers, Gavin, or I'll have my attorney draw up divorce papers tomorrow."

Conflict covers Gavin's face. I'm not sure how the guy is as a father, but as a husband, he's a piece of shit.

*Will he be willing to say good-bye to his child?*

All he seems to care about are games of manipulation. He's most likely using being the father as an excuse to get Grace back because not once has he asked about the baby's well-being.

"Think of what you could do with ten grand," I say, going with my next strategy. "That's a lot of money."

"He'll do it," Vivica bursts out, grabbing a pen from her purse on the entryway table. She smacks Gavin's cheeks a few times as if to wake him up and hands him the pen.

He slowly grabs it. She rifles through the pages until she gets to the last one and pounds her finger against the dotted line. With a sad nod, Gavin signs ... and I nearly fall down in relief.

---

ONE MORE STOP.

One more stop until I can go home to my girl.

I wasn't sure if I'd go through with it. It's a stretch, and it could disappoint me if it doesn't work out. But since I'm on a roll, I might as well keep going until everything is lined up.

I take the steps up to my apartment two at a time. My dad and I have only talked a few times since the night Grace had her nightmare. I've been so busy with figuring shit out with us and helping to get the townhome baby ready. He hasn't asked me for money—*shocker*. Worry hits me when I open the door. I never know what I'll walk into with my father, so I'm expecting a trashed place and an even more trashed father.

The TV is on, and when I walk into the living room, a man is sitting on the couch, sipping on a Pepsi.

"Who the fuck are you?"

I made it clear to my father that I didn't want any of his friends inside my apartment. He can take that shit somewhere else because the last thing I want to worry about is drugs here or people stealing my shit.

The guy smiles up at me. "I'm Darryl." His voice is friendly, not slurred—a first for one of my dad's friends. He's also not high ... and he's dressed in clean clothes.

*What the hell is going on here?*

"Where's my father?" I grit out.

The guy might not be high, but I'm still suspicious.

"In the shower." Darryl places his Pepsi on a coaster on the coffee table.

I scratch my head. "Why are you here?"

"Your father is riding with me to our meeting and seems to be running late. I told him to take his time, and he told me I could wait in here."

My head spins. "Meeting? Meeting for what?"

His face falls. "He still hasn't told you?"

"Hasn't told me what?"

"I think it's best you have that conversation with him."

With perfect timing, my father walks out of the bedroom, buttoning up his shirt.

He smiles. "Oh, hey, son. I see you've met Darryl."

I raise my brows. "I have, and he said you're going to some *meeting*?"

Darryl stands. "I'll wait outside. Give you two some privacy to talk."

I rub the back of my neck.

*What the fuck is going on?*

*What kind of meetings would my dad be attending?*

I inspect my dad, taking in his kempt appearance. He's put on weight and is obviously freshly showered. His words were clear.

He stands inches from me, crossing and then uncrossing his

arms. "I'm attending meetings ... addiction support groups ... to help me sober up. Darryl is my sponsor."

"To help you sober up ... or are you sober?"

He gleams with pride. "I've been sober seven days now. I know it's not much, but it's a start."

I've never felt so much damn pride in my life. "Seriously?"

He nods, his smile filled with just as much pride. "Yes, son."

I smile, yet it's still reserved. "That's fucking awesome, Dad. I'm so proud of you."

He's never done this before. Anytime I've mentioned him getting help or seeing a therapist, he's always insisted he doesn't need help ... that those people don't know what they're talking about.

"What made you decide to do this?" I ask, retreating a step.

"You. My life. Seeing the disgust you had when you picked me up at that house." He gestures to my apartment. "Seeing how living in a nice place can be. I went to the bar, and Archer wouldn't tell me where your new job was." His face falls. "That hurt ... but what really hurt was when I was leaving. Someone stopped and congratulated me on becoming a grandfather soon." His chest hitches. "I had no idea, and as I sat in my car, angry at first, then I burst into tears. That's when it finally hit me. Why would you want someone like me around your baby? I was a piece-of-shit father to you and was still acting irresponsibly. I sat there for an hour, thinking about being a grandfather, and my heart lit up, son. It was like a sign of me needing to get my shit together, so I can be a good grandfather."

*Whoa.*

*This isn't what I expected.*

I came here to tell my father he could stay in the apartment but that he would need to find work and get himself some help. I was on the fence about whether to disclose the baby information to him.

"I'm proud of you." His voice chokes up. "Now, it's time for you to be proud of me. For my grandchild to be proud of me. Please give me a second chance to show you that I can be a better person."

I'm shaking all over, and I shut my eyes.

It's what I wanted from him all along while I was growing up. I was always sad that I wasn't special enough to push him in that direction. It makes me fucking ecstatic that my baby is that important to him to finally take the initiative.

"It's a girl," I state, a wave of heat hitting me as my eyes grow teary. "We're having a baby girl."

"I'm so happy for you, son."

And for the first time, my father and I hug.

# CHAPTER FORTY-ONE

# Grace

GAVIN IS GONE.

The week after the baby shower incident, I was informed my coworkers had signed a petition asking for him to be fired. Since some of my coworkers had been at the shower, they wrote letters to the school board, demanding his temporary replacement become his permanent one. The school board listened, and bye-bye, Gavin.

He's gone from my work. He signed over his parental rights. I blocked his number. My life should be Gavin-free now.

*Good riddance.*

The school day has ended, and there's a spark back in my step—a slow step, given the baby seems to be growing like a weed these days.

I peer up from my desk at a knock on the door to find a nervous Vivica.

*Just when I thought I was Gavin-free.*

"Hear out," Vivica says in one breath.

"How about I show you out?" I counter, gripping my pen so tight that I'm waiting for it to break in half.

"I won't take much of your time," she pleads.

"What do you want?" I uneasily glance around the room, waiting for Gavin to appear ... or something.

*Who even let her in?*

After the show she put on, she should have been banned from stepping foot into this school. Not only that but her husband was also just fired.

She grimaces. "I want to apologize."

I hold my hand up, warding her off from coming closer. "No need."

She holds her belly, which is bigger than mine. She looks ready to give birth at any moment. "That's not my character. I've never done something like that before—not even with Gavin's other mistresses. Maybe it was the pregnancy hormones ... I don't know. Something just snapped inside me."

"I have pregnancy hormones too," I deadpan, not trying to sound like a bitch yet not being overly nice because what she did wasn't cool. "And I found out the father of my child was married, and then he proceeded to practically harass me. Not once did I ever consider treating someone like that, especially someone who hadn't done anything. If you had read my text exchanges with Gavin, you would've seen that I asked him to stop texting, to stop calling, because he was married. No one knew about you until the first day you showed up."

She recoils at my words, but they needed to be said.

I take a steeling breath. "You deserve someone better than him, Vivica. I hope you realize that for the sake of yourself ... and the sake of your family."

Her face tenses. "You know nothing about my personal life. I came here to apologize. I did. Thank you for getting those papers drawn up and the money. I believe that you didn't know, and I appreciate you ending the affair when you found out. Now, we're just looking for the next step. It seems everywhere we go, my husband can't keep his dick in his pants." The last statement is said with a snarl. "I wish you luck, Grace."

"You too, Vivica."

She's sure as hell going to need more than luck.

Maybe a frying pan to whack Gavin over the head and knock some sense into him.

When she disappears through the door, I grab my bag and go home to a man who can keep his dick in his pants.

To Finn.

The man I love.

# CHAPTER FORTY-TWO

# Finn

"I'LL NEVER GET ENOUGH of you," I say to Grace as I kiss up her thigh.

She woke up crampy and nauseous and called off work. I did the same to cater to her. I made her favorite meal and gave her a massage ... which led to now—my face inches from her pussy and my mouth watering. If all else fails, an orgasm always makes my girl feel better.

Before devouring her, I plant a quick kiss on her belly—one of my favorite things to do. The due date is close. The baby bag is packed and at the door. A car seat is strapped into each of our cars. We're ready for our little one to come. At least, we think we are. Neither one of us knows what to expect. Sure, we've read the baby books, attended classes, and been given advice from our friends. But I don't think any of those one hundred percent prepare you for having a baby. I told Grace we'll learn as we go, we don't have to be perfect, and we will make an amazing team.

"Another go at inducing labor?" Grace asks, laughing while staring down at me.

We've had sex—lots and lots of sex—and blame it on attempting to induce labor.

The real reason, though, is we love being intimate with each other. Holding hands, kissing, sex, whatever it is, I love it with Grace.

Her thighs shake at my first lick up her slit. I love how sensitive she is to me. Squirming underneath me, she moans my name as I softly circle her clit with my thumb and navigate my tongue in and out of her. As she gasps and when I know she's getting close, I shove two fingers inside her, working her the way she loves to be worked. In our months of dating, I've learned what Grace likes … and what she looks like when she's about to orgasm.

I quicken my pace, slamming my fingers in and out of her, and she begs for more.

My attention moves away from her thighs to her eyes when she clutches my wrist.

"I need you inside me," she begs. "I need more."

"Come on my tongue, and then I'll give you this cock," I demand, raising my mouth to suck on her clit while finger-fucking her. "And then I'll come inside you."

My words set her on fire, and seconds later, her back arches. I devour her, loving the way her pussy tightens against my fingers, and my cock jerks in my pants, knowing he's next in line. Drawing back, I crawl off the bed, unbutton my pants, and slide them down my legs.

"Uh … Finn," Grace says as I pull my shirt over my head.

I toss it across the room. "Yeah, baby?"

She points at where I just was. "I think my water just broke."

# CHAPTER FORTY-THREE

# Grace

MILLIE ANGELINE DUKE.

My daughter.

*Our* daughter.

I love that she has Finn's last name. With my family's exper-
tise in law, they were able to get that done for us. Finn is her
father, and I wouldn't want it any other way.

I'd asked him to take a few days to think about it before
agreeing to it. It's a big deal—an eighteen-year commitment.
But Finn said he's all in—forever.

I'm exhausted, and I've attempted to rest as the nurses have
told me to do. The ten hours of labor was hard on me—
mentally and physically—but I forgot all about that when they
handed me my beautiful little girl. Six pounds and four ounces
of perfection were finally mine to hold after talking to her
through my skin for so long. I was terrified of motherhood, but
now, I want nothing more than to be the perfect mother to my
little girl.

I cried. Finn cried. Faith cried. Millie cried.

The delivery room was one giant sob-fest.

While Faith had been a good source of mental support in

the room, Finn was my right-hand man. The best partner a pregnant woman could have.

He accepted my verbal abuse.

*"You eat that cheeseburger in front of me, and you'll never eat one again."*

*"Tell me it's easy to push again, and I'm pushing you out that window."*

The poor guy held my hand while I practically ripped his off while crying out in pain. But he'd never walked away, never looked at me any different.

I'm also sure whatever he saw the doctor working with down in my nether regions wasn't a pretty sight. I'd be surprised if he wants to put his face down there again.

*RIP, oral orgasms.*

The baby classes had paid off. Finn was my comfort blanket while I gave birth. He knew what to say and do to keep me going. He had been my comfort blanket during my entire pregnancy really. I'm not sure if I could've done it without him.

Finn sits in the chair next to me, cradling Millie in his arms. As I lay my head back, my mind wanders to the day we decided to pretend. I couldn't have known it would be the best thing I'd ever done. It was always supposed to be Finn.

He was always supposed to be my lover, the father of my child—and from the comments he keeps making, my husband. He's brought up marriage more times than I can count, but I told him that we needed to have our baby first, and then wedding talk could start. Heat radiates through my chest at the thought of being his wife.

"She's beautiful," Finn says, his gaze sliding away from Millie to me. "Just like her mother." He runs his finger along her face. "She has your eyes."

That heat turns ice-cold. I wish I could do what he just did. I'd love to examine Millie and point out every similarity she has to Finn, but I can't. I hate that dread crawls up my throat and ruins this happy moment. Millie won't resemble Finn because she's not his. It's a tough pill to swallow and one I'll have to digest myself. It'd kill me to ever bring it up to Finn.

Biologically, he might not be Millie's father.

But in every other way, he is.

There's a knock on the door, and as soon as I call, "Come in," it flies open.

"Where is my goddaughter?" Georgia sings before holding up a gift bag. "I have presents on presents on presents to give her."

Lola nudges her with her elbow. "I think you mean, *my* goddaughter."

They've been arguing over who the godmother will be for weeks now. Each of them bringing me sweets to sway me in their favor.

I laugh. "How many times have I said that you're both the godmothers?"

"Is that a thing?" Georgia asks. "Can there be two? And if there's two, who's number one?" She sets the bag down on the small couch in the corner. "If so, I'm number one."

A line forms behind the girls. It feels good, having my friends here. Georgia texted an hour ago, making sure I was ready for people, and I replied that I was. I want the people I care about to meet my little one.

Cassidy waddles in and looks straight at me. "Don't tell me any horror stories, please. Lincoln has made me watch birthing pregnancy videos, and I'm terrified."

Finn chuckles. "Prepare yourself for war, Lincoln."

"Hardy-har-har," I grumble.

Georgia is the first to ask to hold Millie because she's Georgia, and she always has to be the first in line. Nervously, I tell her to take a seat as if she were a child holding a new puppy, and I instruct Finn to carefully place her in Georgia's arms. I give Georgia directions on how to hold her, to protect her head

—nearly everything the nurses said to me. I'm going to tell anyone else who asks to hold her the same. It's only been two days, and I know I'll do anything to protect my little girl.

There are so many things I can't wait for—to take her home, to change her diapers regularly (weird, I know), and to give her as much love as I can.

I think back to how this day might have been if it had been Gavin with me here and shudder. I'd have kicked him out of the room. The next thought that swims through my brain is having to do it alone without Finn. The thought nearly pulls tears from my eyes. Millie deserves the perfect family, and that's what we'll give her.

Not a half-assed dad.

A family to love her, to want her, to put her first.

I'll never worry about the issues Vivica has to worry about. Finn would never cheat, never turn his back on us, and never put himself before his family. I have a good man.

By the time everyone leaves, I'm exhausted. That doesn't stop me from cradling my daughter to my chest as I doze off to sleep. This is my new life, and I can't wait for the journey it takes me on.

# Finn

"THAT'S the hottest thing I've ever laid eyes on."

My gaze sweeps over to Grace sitting on the bed. "Huh?"

She gestures to Millie in my arms. "You, shirtless, sexy, wearing gray sweats while holding our baby." She licks her lips. "I always thought you were hot, but this is like an orgasm." She pouts. "The only orgasm I'll have for a minute."

I chuckle. "Now, do you understand all those times I told you that motherhood looks sexy as fuck on you?"

"Yeah, yeah, yeah," she mutters. "You told me how sexy I was when I was like a stuffed turkey."

Tonight is Millie's first day home. Our friends wanted to throw a welcome-home party, of course, but we told them to wait until the weekend. Not only do Grace and I need time to adjust, but so does Millie. Even after such a short time, I love this little girl. Grace allowing me into their lives is a fucking blessing I'll never take for granted.

I inspect her in my arms. She's so tiny but already weighs down my heart. She yawns, her tongue sticking out, before shutting her eyes again. I tiptoe to her bassinet, kiss her forehead, and carefully lay her down, making sure she's lying exactly how we were instructed she needed to be. As I climb back into bed with Grace, I think about having more babies with her.

No matter what, Millie will always be my daughter. When I confided in Cohen about taking on the rights as her father, he asked if I'd ever tell Millie the truth about her biological father. I gulp, thinking about when that day would possibly come. It's hard to know the future, but I hope I never have to disclose that information to her. Grace and I made a pact; albeit some might think it's selfish of us, as far as Millie will ever know, I'm her dad.

I pull Grace into my arms. "How are you feeling, baby?"

"Exhausted but happy ..." She sighs. "Content. You?"

"The happiest I've ever been."

Grace and I took the long route in our relationship, but the greatest things often take time, right? Like fine wine, it only gets better. For years, we chased the dream of a relationship but never fully jumped in. It's been a marathon, but I'm glad I never stopped chasing her, happy I never gave up.

We're done chasing each other.

Chasing our feelings.

We've caught the love of our lives.

And now, we're a family.

---

**I hope you enjoyed Finn and Grace's story!** There's so much more in the Twisted Fox series with other characters getting their own HEA. All books can be read as standalones. I'd love for you to join me for Silas and Lola's story, Last Round!

# KEEP UP WITH THE TWISTED FOX SERIES

*If you enjoyed Finn and Grace's story, check out the other books in the Twisted Fox series!*

**Stirred**
(Cohen & Jamie's story)
**Shaken**
(Archer & Georgia's story)
**Straight Up**
(Lincoln & Cassidy's story)
**Chaser**
(Finn & Grace's story)
**Last Round**
(Silas and Lola's story)

# ALSO BY CHARITY FERRELL

## TWISTED FOX SERIES

(each book can be read as a standalone)

Stirred

Shaken

Straight Up

Chaser

Last Round

## BLUE BEECH SERIES

(each book can be read as a standalone)

Just A Fling

Just One Night

Just Exes

Just Neighbors

Just Roommates

Just Friends

## STANDALONES

Bad For You

Beneath Our Faults

Pop Rock

Pretty and Reckless

Revive Me

Wild Thoughts

**RISKY DUET**

Risky

Worth The Risk

# ABOUT THE AUTHOR

Charity Ferrell resides in Indianapolis, Indiana with her future hubby and two fur babies. She loves writing about broken people finding love with a dash of humor and heartbreak, and angst is her happy place.

When she's not writing, she's making a Starbucks run, shopping online, or spending time with her family.

Visit my website:
www.charityferrell.com